Sile... is the
Crown

the boss had a go at signing too!

Thank you for entering the 1 year gweaway! I hope you enjoy!

MJ Weatherall

First Published in 2021 by Blossom Spring
Publishing
Silent is the Crown Copyright © 2021

MJ Weatherall

ISBN 978-1-8382421-8-3

E: admin@blossomspringpublishing.com

W: www.blossomspringpublishing.com

Acknowledgments

For my baby sister, Eliza. Who is and always will be my number one fan.

For Sammy, without your support and advice this wouldn't be possible. Thank you for believing in me, especially when I didn't believe in myself.

And to all the others I have met on the way, those that have inspired, nurtured and driven me (even if they didn't mean to). Thank you.

Chapter One
The Girl

What am I doing here? What is this place? Who am I? Many questions arose in the girls' head as she woke up, sunlight blinding her delicate grey eyes. She was laying on the floor of a clearing that was steeped in autumnal colours. Shed leaves from the surrounding trees coated the floor around the girl, who was damp with morning dew. She looked around the clearing, studying its every inch, branch and leaf.

The clearing was large, with patches of grass and wildflowers swimming in the centre, larger shrubs and young-looking trees surrounded it. The girl didn't know how long she had observed the forest for, its colours and diversity blinded her with information and her imagination ran wild. She imagined pixies and fairies dancing amongst the mornings sunbeams, darting happily from flower to flower and tree to tree with no care in the world but to enjoy nature and all their bountiful days.

She was pulled from this beautiful fantasy world suddenly when she realised that she was being watched, the hairs on her neck stood on end. A small elderly woman garbed in plain clothes hovered just out of plain sight near the edge of the clearing, she was too far away for the girl to have seen her features clearly but she knew from the long silvery hair that she must have been elderly and guessed from her stature that she must have been a woman.

Her almost white locks contrasted dramatically against the broad oak tree she had been leaning on, she hadn't reacted when the girl saw her, she had just continued to stare, to watch, to wait. Then she slowly turned and walked away as if the girl hadn't been there, as if she hadn't seen her in the first place… as if the girl had been a ghost.

The girl gasped, then slowly looked down at her porcelain white hands and examined them as if she was unsure herself if she had been there, she had grasped and nipped her pale skin until she was sure she was alive and only when her pale skin had begun to turn red, then purple had she been completely sure.

After sitting in the clearing observing the world for a while longer, til the sun had risen above her and the heat of the day should have warmed through her bones, she realised she was cold and wasn't going to warm up. She shivered and rose to her feet. *Who was that woman? Where do I go now? Who am I?* She'd hugged her arms close to her body and hoped that she might conserve some heat but she had only been a small, thin child and hadn't much insulation for cold days. She had looked down at the clothes she was wearing, a plain grey dress that had delicate white embroidery on the cuffs. The girl scowled, her clothes clearly hadn't been designed for this sort of weather and had done her no favours.

She looked over to where the woman had stood and sighed, the woman had just disappeared into thin air and the girl hadn't seen her since, *maybe the woman was the ghost?* The girl thought, as she briskly walked over to the broad oak. She had been half-way to the oak when she realised that she was bare-foot, the long wet grass had tickled the bottom of her soft pale feet with every step. She had walked more carefully after that and picked her way around the briars and nettles, determined to get to the place where the only other person she had seen in this world had been.

Why can't I remember anything about my life? I must have a name, what is my name? Who am I? Engrossed in thought and with questions spinning around her young mind, the girl had accidentally stepped on a briar with needle-like thorns that had pierced the soft white flesh of her bare foot. She gasped in pain and reached down to her foot, the shock of the event caused her to immediately lose balance and she had fallen into a slightly longer patch of grass away from the briars. Wet from the morning dew on the grass the girl scowled again, she was still seated, uncomfortably, when she wiped the beading crimson blood from her foot and plucked a few tiny thorns from her flesh, she grimaced, *why did they hurt more coming out than they did going in?* She had stopped when she heard a distant noise. A soft tapping, getting closer and it had got louder with each passing second. Subconsciously the girl had known that sound, the girl panicked and ducked down into the long grass and peered slyly towards where the noise had come from, she pushed her jet black hair from her eyes so that she had the perfect view, she hadn't wanted to miss anything going on in her small edge of the world. She had realised again, that she had been wandering around all day without having a recollection of who she was, where she was from or anything that might give her some idea as to the life she had lived before. Because she had woken up in the clearing all those hours previously, she hadn't had time to dwell on that depressing fact, and now, fast approaching was something unknown to her, which could have been anything at that point.

The tapping had become louder and louder, closer and closer; and soon a man stood there in the road with half of his body hidden by long grass. He hadn't been a particularly handsome man, the girl thought, but he looked kind. Maybe it was meant to happen and she was supposed to be found by this man and his cart, perhaps he would help her figure out who she was and take her home to her family. Many thoughts swirled in her head as she began to rise to her feet.

Reality came crashing down on her as two strong bony hands pulled her back to the damp ground in desperation. In awe at her own stupidity, the girl remained on the ground un-resisting. She turned slightly to look behind her and saw the woman from earlier laid, her bony arms still clutching the young girl to her like a mother with a new-born babe. The woman raised a single bony finger to her lips and then slowly, as if any movement could alert the man to their location, she pointed back towards the man, gesturing for her to watch the events about to unfold.

The girl focused on the man once more, his soft brown hair falling in curls by his ears, his beard kempt and soft looking, his clothes looked in much better condition than the ones the girl herself wore. *The man was clearly rich,* the girl thought. More and more questions surged around the girl's head as she watched the man from her skeleton prison in the grass, *who was this woman and why does she want to protect me from this man? Why should I trust anyone that I have just met including this old harpy embracing me? Who the heck am I and why can't I remember anything?*

The man was talking to someone out of sight of the girl and the woman's hiding place, it took most of the girls will power to resist the urge to crane her neck to see who the man was gesturing so wildly to.

"What's taking you so long?" Said the kempt man in

anguish. "The King wants these slaves to be at the castle before nightfall! And we are still half a day's ride away!"

"What d'you want me to do milord, they won't move 'ny faster, they're tired 'n hungry." A weaker voice replied.

The girl looked back towards the old woman with a questioning look on her pale face. *Slaves? Castle? King?* Her brain whirred, she definitely had to get her memories back because each second was agonisingly packed with new information. The elderly woman ignored the inquisitive look on the girl's face and just hardened her stare towards the kempt man as if to say 'watch this'.

As quickly as they had arrived, the man, along with his small procession disappeared down the road and out of sight and earshot of the girl and her saviour, taking their slaves and confusion with them, leaving the girl tired and confused in their wake.

In the aftermath of the encounter, the girl turned to face the old woman, determined to say thank you and to ask for the woman's help in figuring out the world and her place in it. That was when the girl realised that she hadn't felt the bony arms unwind themselves from her torso, she didn't hear the soft pattering of leather shoes on the grass as the woman sneaked away for the second time that day, because she was no longer there.

Dejected and alone the girl remained on the floor amongst the long grass until the sun began to set. She was increasingly worried by the darkening of the sky, the lengthening of the shadows and the creeping of the nocturnal animals out of their homes. She tried to call out for the woman, but her voice wasn't there. She tried to form words like those she had heard on the

5

road not that long ago but she could not remember how, she could see them in her mind but she could not make her throat speak them. She couldn't remember anything, not even how to speak.

After this dark realisation the world became a darker and scarier place for the girl, who had no recollection of the night and had no one to guide her through all the parts of life she was struggling with. She cried soundlessly for most of the night, buried in the long grass with the hope that the soft green blades would act as some kind of protection from the screeching, squawking, howling creatures of the darkness.

Her heart began to pound in her ears, the world began to spin with fear; of the darkness, of the creatures that lurked within it and the fear that she was perpetually alone. She shivered, the cold penetrating her thin dress and straight into her bones, she closed her eyes and hoped for it all to end.

***

The girl awoke with the morning sunbeams dancing across her pale, tear stained face. The trees were swaying softly in the wind, no sign of the night remained, no sound like those evil screeches lingered. She had drifted off to sleep eventually when the crying and shivering had exhausted her; she had only woken again because of the gut wrenching, gnawing pain in her stomach. *Am I dying? Am I dead already? Did I die in the darkness? Who am I? Who was I?* The girls groggy morning thoughts confused her slightly as she opened her eyes, blinking the fresh dew and sunlight out with her long black eyelashes.

She rose achily to her feet, once more doused in the morning dew that slaked the ground. She walked to the edge of the clearing, stretching the aches and pains from her muscles and the cold from her bones with every stride, she walked to the place by the side of the road where the man was before. A worn streak of land disappearing into the distance lay on either side of the girl. *Which way is the right way?* the girl thought to herself desperately *and which way did that man go?* Something that was an afterthought surfaced in her brain like a predator pouncing on its prey. Scary, sudden and surprising, the girl tried to push the thought away, but it had already rooted itself in her brain, it rooted there the moment the man disappeared from her view.

She looked from one end of the road to the other with the clearing behind her, *left went deeper into the forest by the looks of things,* thought the girl; through Oak, Alder, Beech and Birch trees alike, all looming, waiting for her to put one wrong foot off the path before they grabbed, tore and ripped into her, like the creatures of the night had wanted to.

The path to the right was more open, like the clearing she had once felt so comfortable in, but had also felt unprotected and vulnerable, a ready meal for any creature or vagabond wanting to gobble her up or murder her.

The decision was too hard for the girl, she was stressed and exhausted after the previous day's events, she had never had to deal with something so life changing and important before and she had no memories to help her with the decision. She kept thinking about the man and how if she came across any people she would not be able to talk to them and that would make it even harder to find her family and wherever she was meant to be.

Eventually the girl decided to go right, towards the open fields and meadows where she could walk without feeling trapped and oppressed. She walked on the well-trodden path which was easier on her bare feet than the clearing due to the lack of briars and nettles. She found her gaze moving from her feet and the ground, to her surroundings which were still lit by the early morning rays and dappled with a cool mist. Bushes of brilliant black berries coated the left side of the path, whilst the right side still lead to the clearing, adorned by trees that stood to attention like palace guards but like the girl had found out, did not serve much protection. At the sight of the juicy berries her stomach growled fiercely once more, the gnawing pain made her double over shakily. She needed to eat soon otherwise she might become the ghost that she had feared she was the day before, forever haunting the earth silently searching for her long lost family.

With this in mind the girls' eye was once again drawn to the deep black berries which clung to nearby bushes, inviting her to sample their juicy soft flesh, the girl closed in on one of the bushes hungrily. She rolled one of the midnight black berries between her thumb and forefinger and pierced it inquisitively with her thumbnail. Purple juice ran down the digit and pooled in the palm of her hand. She licked the juice hungrily. It was bitter at first and then after a few seconds of peace and satisfaction, it began to sting and burn the girls throat like acid, she gasped and dropped the remnants of the offending berry, clutching at her throat with ivory fingers.

Panting heavily, still clutching her throat with her head bent towards the ground, the girl opened her eyes. She was surprised to see a pair of shoes in front of her, small brown leather things with a darker leather binding. The girl looked up to see the owner of the shoes and was surprised to see it was the old woman from before. She tried once more to speak but could not. The old woman shook her head sadly and reached out with those long bony fingers to grab the girl's youthful pale wrist and pulled her along the path after her.

"You have much to learn, my girl." Was all she said as she led the girl along the beaten track, past the clearing and deep into the woods. Leaving the spring smells of the clearing behind them.

The girl was half pulled, half dragged behind the woman who was surprisingly strong and fast for her advanced age. The girl also noticed that while she appeared elderly at first glance she was much taller and stronger than the girl had expected her to be, she was more than a head taller than her. The girl could not see much of the path that she was stumbling down for her inky black hair flapped in front of her eyes like a thick curtain. She had no idea where the woman was taking her but she didn't feel like she was in any immediate danger, unlike when the man with his cart had almost seen her or when that black berry had almost killed her.

It felt like forever until the woman finally stopped walking and the bony handcuff released the girl, who then pushed the hair out of her face and looked up. Through a hazy vision she gazed upon a small cottage with a beautiful, thatched roof, homely vegetables grew just out front and several chickens clucked and cooed as they pecked around the place.

The girl managed to smile at the woman, who had

wandered in through the open front door of the cottage. The girl waited for a moment to see if she was going to reappear but curiosity and a smell that was causing her stomach to go crazy got the better of her and she walked into the cottage through the open door just as the woman had done minutes before.

She tried to take in everything she could see but the sights were overwhelming, herbs hanging from the ceiling, an invitingly warm fire in the fireplace, a cooking pot over the flames, shelves upon shelves of jars filled with preserves and other concoctions, a black cat squinting coyly from the rafters, recently used pots and pans piled up in the sink. The last thing that the girl noticed in the room, where the two other elderly women that stood with hands on their hips frozen like statues, staring at what their companion had dragged into their home. At the sight of them the girl stopped looking about the place immediately and lowered her eyes modestly to the table, she stood still while the women continued to glare at her furiously.

The woman that had brought the girl to the cottage began whirling around the kitchen, clattering pots and pans, picking up spices and a random assortment of other ingredients that were to hand. She did this all in silence, ignoring the petrified stares of the two other women. When she'd finished she turned back to the girl, she held a bowl of piping hot soup in one hand and a spoon in the other. She set the bowl and a spoon in front of the skinny girl.

"Eat up." She said, eagerly eyeing the soup. The girl did as she was told, hungrily spooning mouthfuls of the wonderful liquid into her mouth, now almost unaware of her observers.

"What have you brought this wretch here for?" Said

one of the women, the stern looking one with the dark brown dress, neat hair and a tightly drawn mouth.

"She's lost, can't speak and tried to eat belladonna. What else was I supposed to do, Maple?" Said the woman who'd brought the girl to the cottage.

"Hazel does have a point you know, Maple." Said the last woman, who was smaller, stouter and had a kinder, rounder face than the other two. "She's such a pretty young thing, beautiful black hair. She sure would brighten up the place."

"You always take her side, Juniper!" Maple hissed, staring from Hazel to Juniper in disgust.

"Does she have a name?" Juniper asked inquisitively, wandering over to the girl and examining her more closely like cattle she was planning to buy at auction.

"Doesn't speak." Said Hazel, busying herself with the cooking pot over the fire.

"What shall we call her then?" Juniper inquires, pulling small leaves out of the girl's hair.

"She isn't a cat, Juniper!" Maple hissed once more, the mere presence of the girl clearly upsetting the woman.

"Yes but she has to have a name doesn't she? We can't just keep calling her *the girl* can we?" Maple retorted with colour rushing quickly to her chubby cheeks, clearly she wasn't used to being spoken to like that in front of guests.

"Belladonna." Said Hazel. All three women turned to look at the scrawny, starving, unkempt girl, sat at their kitchen table and said in unison.

"Belladonna."

And that was how the girl got her name.

Chapter Two
New Beginnings

The lonely, young, abandoned girl that woke up one morning in a clearing with no memories was neither lonely nor without memories, for she had spent a year with three elderly foragers in a cottage in the forest. She was named Belladonna after the poisonous but beautiful and alluring plant, she spent her time learning about sustainable living and the ways of the world. With her aging guardians she collected wild plants to make medicines, food and tools. Belladonna watched them and helped whenever she could, even though she was still a young girl and Maple still hadn't warmed to her; despite the fact she had been living in the cottage for well over a year.

Hazel taught Belladonna many things during that first year that both interested and excited her, everything was new to her and she found that because she had spent her first few days with no memories or information, she had a thirst for knowledge and wanted to know everything there was to know about everything. Including how to be a young lady, because one day, the women told her, she might have to leave the cottage and would maybe want to marry, and for that she had to be a presentable young lady to fit in with the society and politics of the Kingdom. They also taught her how to cook and clean so that she never had to depend on anyone else to keep her alive, how to read and write so that she could communicate, but they could never teach her how to speak no matter how hard they tried and how many different techniques and herbal concoctions they had devised.

This was devastating for Belladonna, she had always thought that she would be able to get her voice back and that the women, who were the most intelligent people she thought she would ever meet, would be the people that would be able to heal her. She didn't know how old she was because she had no real concept of time yet and no memories to be able to form a guess but the three women, with all their years of experience believed she was eight years old when she came to them. They also believed that she was a mute and would likely never speak again, if she had ever spoken in the first place.

***

Belladonna was sat at the kitchen table that she had long been accustomed to and fondly watched her three guardians bustling about the kitchen, crushing herbs, mixing poultices, and cooking supper just like they did every day. She had grown used to the women's chatter over the duration of her stay with them and listened to it carelessly and automatically, it became a comfortable background noise that accompanied her studies. She listened a lot, she was good at it.

From her seat at the kitchen table Belladonna could hear that there was more noise than usual from the road outside the cottage, a great number of hoof beats and footsteps pattering quickly against the dusty road surface. She rose from her seat as what sounded like a herd, grew closer. She banged on the table sharply to get the women's attention.

"What is it?" Said Maple, as warm as ever towards the girl. But Belladonna ignored her and began writing, scribbling furiously, nearly ripping the paper with her pen, she held it up to the women in anguish. As she had been writing the noise grew louder and she hadn't really given the women an advantage because in the silence of the bustling kitchen, they could all hear it.

"Well done girl." Maple directed at the girl and then turned swiftly to her companions, not appearing to be too rattled by the events unfolding "There may be a mob outside, the girl must go."

Belladonna was in shock, that wasn't what she meant at all, she didn't want to be sent away from the cottage. Juniper looked at the girl sadly, but the look on her face showed her that she wasn't going to fight Maple on the matter, this time.

"Bella, Maple's right. It's not safe for you here anymore, we have taught you all we can and I am confident that you will survive in this world. Which is much better than when you came to us. Our job is done." Hazel said, leaning down and taking the girls hands in her own bony calloused ones one last time. Her eyes shimmering with emotion like Belladonna had never seen before, a sob caught in the girl's throat as she embraced her elderly mentor for what she believed would be the last time.

Juniper pulled out a bag from under the floorboards, held it gingerly for a second as if weighing it and then passed it over to the girl.

"Everything you may need is in here, I wish you the best of luck, don't look back." Juniper said, a single tear ran its course down her tanned wrinkled face, she awkwardly hugged the girl tight, the bag in the middle pressing painfully into the girl's ribs. She wasn't bothered about the pain from the bag though because the pain of having to leave her home and her adoptive family was much worse.

Belladonna swung the bag over her shoulders in order to distribute the weight of the numerous jars and other supplies evenly, she looked questioningly at Hazel, who like the other two women were busy tidying things in kitchen, hiding some of the more dubious items and who like the other two hadn't been able to give her an explanation for what was going on and why they were so calm about it.

"We knew this day would come, three old women living and working together in the woods as foragers and healers, people don't understand! They never have!" Hazel said in reply to the silent question and the piercing stare, she grabbed the girl by the shoulders "You have to go, NOW! There is a mob outside that probably want to burn us all for witchcraft, you must leave, save yourself, they don't know you were ever here. GO." The woman said as she pushed Belladonna out the back door.

Belladonna took one last look at the only home she had ever known, the women that had taught her all she knew and disappeared like a thief in the night into the forest behind the cottage.

Chapter Three
A Tavern of Secrets

Belladonna had lived for many years always wondering about the fate of her three guardians, had they escaped? Or had they fallen victim to a plague of angry villagers that feared an imaginary enemy? Over the years she thought of different scenarios, each less plausible than the last until she made it her mission to find out the truth. The whole truth from the very beginning; the events that led her to wake up in that clearing with memory loss, to find out who she was, who her family were and finally to find out what happened to her childhood guardians and avenge them if necessary.

***

After many years living in uncertainty and poverty on the streets, roaming from town to town, city to city, against all odds Belladonna had managed to survive. She had reached a point in her life where she was once again in control. She had picked up many skills during these years and had been accompanied on her journey by many different companions and mentor figures, all of which had imparted important knowledge with her. Hand to hand combat and self-defence with Striker, lock picking from a friendly thief called Jock who she spent many adrenalin filled heists with, knife combat with Melanie Steepwater, who was by far her favourite mentor. She was ex Castle militia and an all-round badass woman, who Belladonna spent some time with whilst in an edge of the known world type village where chaos reigned. Melanie was the local militia leader of Northern Skyole, which had no funding from the Castle because it was so close to the dread zone, it was a small gang of enforcers in a near lawless county.

Belladonna had many fond memories of Melanie but the one that had stuck with her the most was the battle for the Edonian border. She could remember it as clearly as if it had happened yesterday. Melanie Steepwater stood garbed head to toe in the finest gold plate armour. Its designs were so intricate and beautiful that it looked like it had no place on the battlefield. She had looked out amongst the edge lands, the last place where humans dared to set foot before the dread zone, her emerald eyes burning with such a ferocity Bella had never seen before. Such ferocity she had later come to learn masked deep pain.

Melanie rose her sword in the air and looked back at her rag tag army, the last line of defence and the bravest group of people Bella had ever known.

"Today we fight, not for our King and not for our Gods. Today we fight for men and women! People we have lost, for the people we are scared we might lose still and people who don't even know we exist. So today my friends, my family, my soldiers, we fight and we win!!" Her voice rang out followed by a cheer and a rhythmic stamping of feet, a banging of swords on shields and a low throaty chant to create an illusion of thousands of marching soldiers, whether that was the intention or not. The battle cry had succeeded in its purpose and caused a new wave of energy in the small army.

Melanie turned to wink at Bella, who had been standing on the front line of the small army (which was only around two hundred strong made up of the local militia and anyone they could convince to put on armour and carry a sword). Melanie had been her hero for some time before that day, but after what she had witnessed on that battlefield that day, she worshipped her like a God.

Bella remembered that everyone had been opposed to her being on the battlefield that day but once they had seen her in combat, they had swiftly changed their minds, even at the age of twelve she was a better swordsman than most of the men standing round her. She had to be, she didn't have their strength or their experience.

A returning battle cry came from the woods opposite, just like Melanie thought they would. It was a blood curdling screech that ripped from the throats of the mutated. This had been the first time Bella laid eyes upon the mutants and she'd never forget it. They were like people, only their hairless skin looked mottled and melted, they either had too many or not enough limbs and the thing that scared Bella the most was that they had no eyes. It wasn't like whoever created them had forgotten to give them eye sockets, with soft fleshy eye balls nestled within them, it was like they had melted out of their heads and rolled down their cheeks, like tears should have.

After that battle Belladonna had toured most of the rediscovered world looking for a place to fit in, a place where she could settle down and get on with her life but she never found a place where she'd wanted to stay. Partly because of the niggling feeling in the back of her brain that said *if you keep going you might find your family, you might finally find some answers* or *is this really what you want to do with your life, settle down here and be bored?* So she kept on moving, never staying in one place long enough to get comfortable or create relationships that she couldn't bear to leave behind. She hated it, but she hated the thought of never knowing who she was more which is what motivated her to keep moving.

Six years after her escape from the mob, she accidentally returned to the village near where she lived with the three women all those years ago. She found herself in the village she'd never learnt the name of and hadn't been able to find her way back to in all her years of travelling, she found herself sat at the bar of a small tavern called the Kings Head (named for reasons you can probably imagine). They said that the previous King had been usurped because of his obsession with witchcraft which made the people believe that he was mad and the reason he was beheaded. What Belladonna thought was especially hypocritical was even into the new Kings reign some men still took it upon themselves to murder *witches* in their villages, which she'd decided was just them using witchcraft as an excuse to off women they didn't like. Bella always tried to stay away from politics as she travelled too often to be properly invested in the local squabbles but there was something almost universal about men's hatred for intelligent women, those deemed witches, it was something that resonated with her on a deeply personal level and whether it was out of sheer boredom and lack of direction or the need to avenge her guardians, she could never be sure how her quest had started.

At the bar she had overheard a couple of bar flies talking about a meeting that some of the local men were having in the back room of the tavern later that night, a witch hunters meeting.

"Don't know why they bother anymore." Said one

of the drunken men, who was nursing a tankard of ale to his chest, his eyes focussed longingly on the back of the bar where the bottles of the stronger stuff was kept.

"No one's going to stop 'em here are they? No one cares." Said the second man who was barely able to stay seated on his bar stool.

"You know I found their clerk's journal after the last time they met, I think he skipped town Merl." Slurred the first drunk. Belladonna was sat at the other end of the bar straining her ears to hear the conversation without attracting attention, she was cradling a tankard of her own, she was dressed in male clothing with a thick hood draped over her head and face. She would have never been allowed into the tavern as a girl and if she was discovered it wasn't likely to end well for her.

"No way, h-he didn't like murdering women folk anymore then, whatcha do wit' the journal Daevy?" Asked Merl, neither were aware of the eavesdropper at the bar, they were probably used to being the only ones in the tavern at that time of the day and didn't take any care in guarding their conversations, no doubt by the time ordinary people entered the tavern they wouldn't be making much sense by that point.

"Here." Daevy replied by plucking a small leather bound journal from the grotesque depths of his trench coat pocket and slamming it drunkenly on the sticky bar in front of Merl. Belladonna smiled under her thick hood and sipped her ale, biding her time. Knowing the men would be easy to fool at this point, she decided to make her move. She had noticed that after every tankard of ale the men had needed to relieve themselves, so she hailed the barman over and ordered the men a drink each. They were too drunk to be suspicious of a beverage from a kindly stranger at the bar, Belladonna smiled darkly to herself under the large hood that concealed her face. She was enjoying herself, this was the most fun she'd had in months. She felt mounting exhilaration at the thought of a new lead.

The men nodded their appreciation towards Bella, the hooded loner who clearly didn't want to engage in conversation. She nodded back and returned to her drink, staring aimlessly at the back of the bar almost exactly like one of the drunks had done, but without the longing he felt to drown his sorrows and escape his sad, mediocre life. After a while Merl belched and slammed his empty tankard on the sticky bar alongside the journal that hadn't moved.

"I need a piss." He said stumbling off the barstool and towards the toilets. Daevy closed his eyes and nodded. Bella was tense and ready to pounce, she was planning on bumping into Daevy on her way to the door and grabbing the journal, he would just think she was drunk and he would think nothing of the journal until after she had left. Lady luck had other plans, Daevy still had his eyes closed and began to lower his head to his arm, which was resting on the bar for support. After roughly a minute he began to snore. Bella figured she'd have seconds before Merl came back from the toilet. Anxious that the barman could turn around at any moment, she went for it, swapping the journal for her empty tankard, she fled the pub like an eerie breeze.

Once outside Belladonna walked through narrow cobbled streets, the sun was still hanging in the sky lazily, it wouldn't go down for hours yet and Belladonna couldn't do what she was planning to do until it was dark. The time when the most unspeakable acts were to be committed, for Belladonna this was the time where she felt the safest, people didn't look at you twice when it was dark. In the day it was a completely different story, people looked at you and judged you, they wondered why they had never seen you before and it made them uncomfortable.

Belladonna decided to come back to the inn after dark when she had read the journal and decided what she was going to do. She needed a plan.

***

Belladonna retracted once more as the man's heavy leathered fist connected with her face, she was tied to a rough wooden chair, heavy rope bound her hands and feet. The room was dark and damp, and full of men that wanted to hear her confess to being a witch. She had managed to infiltrate a secret meeting in the back room of the Kings Head tavern, she had believed it to be going very well. It was almost too easy to make them believe she was a witch, a girl drinking ale alone in a tavern wearing men's clothes was enough to make people assume the most outrageous things. She got the idea earlier in the day when she was eavesdropping on Merl and Daevy, she had thought about what they would have done or said if she had lowered her hood and revealed herself as a girl, would they have even noticed? It had been too easy, she hadn't even had the chance to finish her drink before it all kicked off. She wished now she'd had a chance to finish it, it would have taken the edge off the beating she was receiving.

"I'm going to ask you again," Said the man knelt in front of the chair. His face was weathered with age but he still looked tough despite the fact he only had a few teeth, he had a shaved head and a thick working class stature. *He was probably a blacksmith, a brute with no brains* she thought. "What do you have to say for yourself?" He hissed. The girl spat out a blood-filled splodge that landed on the uneven stone next to the man's knees as her only reply. He leaned closer, he was so close she could feel his rancid tobacco breath on her face. The smell made her nauseous and she retracted slightly trying to get a gulp of fresher air before she vomited. This only made him lean in closer, confidence radiated off him as he sneered at the young, defenceless girl he had tied to a chair. He laughed a mocking confident laugh, which was immediately echoed by the other members of the secret gathering, who appeared to be less certain about beating up a young girl in the back room of a tavern.

The girl smacked her head down, firmly connecting with the blacksmiths (as she had decided to refer to him) nose with a loud *crack!* She had moved so quickly that she was almost a blur to the spectators in the room. The blacksmith cried out furiously with his nose gushing blood freely down his weathered face and tears streaming from his beady black eyes. Belladonna smiled sweetly at the other men in the room making them all feel very uncomfortable, they began fidgeting with unease, until they remembered that she was tied to a chair, that she couldn't possibly hurt them because she was just a little girl, tied to a chair, right? Wrong.

When the confident looks returned to the faces of the men around the room and the unease visibly melted off their features, Belladonna stood up continuing to watch their faces as the ropes they were so confident in, dropped to the ground, almost as quickly as their smiles dropped from their faces.

She stretched her arms out like an eagle taking flight and then took what appeared to be a short bow, Bella had always loved adding a flare of drama into her work, she revelled in the way it portrayed what she was thinking.

Slowly, with every pair of eyes in the room glued to her, she came out of her deep bow, simultaneously pulling a small leather-bound journal from inside her cloak and held it up so that all the men in the room could see it. They all recognised the book and had been wondering what had happened to the man to whom it had previously belonged.

Belladonna then dramatically tore out a black page, striving to keep the attention of the room, then began writing quickly and although written quickly, the words she wrote didn't appear rushed, they were neat, beautiful and chosen carefully. She handed the piece of paper to the man closest to her, well, the closest man to her that wasn't bleeding profusely from his face, a burly man with shoulder length dirty blonde hair, and beckoned him to read it aloud. He cleared his throat and began.

"I was very interested in the contents of the clerk's journal, about your secret Witch Hunters club." He paused as she paced slowly towards the door, captivating her audience even though the words weren't coming from her own mouth. "And it was very interesting to me to find out that against the King's orders, you still burn women you dislike, as witches..."

Having regained himself the blacksmith made a staggered move towards the girl, his sword half drawn in anger and embarrassment, with one flick of Bella's wrist the man collapsed to the floor with blood oozing out of his neck as well as his nose, from the throwing knife embedded there.

The other members of the secret club took one look at the body on the ground and let the girl walk freely to the exit and the man she had chosen to read continued in his reading because he was scared that he too may bleed his life force onto the same stone floor if he didn't.

"If I hear anything that leads me to believe this *club* is meeting again he won't be the only casualty, I can promise you all that. For this you have my silence." She nodded to the reader as she took one last look around the room before reaching for the doorknob with one hand and gripping her dagger with the other.

Once outside she sighed a deep sigh of relief and closed her eyes for a brief second. She knew the blacksmith would go for her again. He couldn't let a young girl embarrass him like that and not try and redeem himself in the eyes of his secret club. She opened her eyes and made her way through the muddy streets leading away from the Kings Head tavern, passing closed shops and empty stalls, in the darkness of the town she had ended up in.

As she walked in silence she reminisced about her first memories, how the darkness had once scared her and that she now thrived in it. She thought about her elderly guardians and how she was forced to escape and make her way in the world at such a young age. She knew she was bound to end up back in the village where it had all started but it still shocked her that it had happened. Saddened by the lack of new information the tavern had brought her. The girl found herself asking the same old questions, although never out loud. *Who am I? Who was I? What really happened to my guardians?*

She walked aimlessly around the streets hoping to remember something that might help her mission, she was so engrossed in thought that she didn't hear the footsteps approach, she only felt a blow to the back of her head and only saw the ground rise up to meet her like an old friend.

Chapter Four
The Guild

When Belladonna awoke all she saw was darkness, black and deep. It felt like her eyes were covered with a thick material designed to shroud her from seeing her attacker. Then she realised that is exactly what it was. Cursing herself for being slow on the uptake and regretting moving her head, she quickly tried to work out who would have had her kidnapped.

"She's awake." A gruff voice said, Bella couldn't pin-point exactly where the speaker was located as the room made sound travel bizarrely. They were probably underground or in a windowless room, she surmised. She tried to move her hands, but they were tied tight. These people weren't messing around, they had bound her hands better than anyone had bound her hands before, ever, and she had been in her fair share of those situations. Other people's fair shares too for that matter.

"You'll have a hard time getting out of them, little miss." Said another voice different from the first, it was softer but potentially had a sharp edge to it. "We know how to tie someone up unlike them buffoons at the tavern, very impressive your stunts in there by the way. Too bad you couldn't have stayed off our radar." The second man continued.

"Shut up, you always say too much." The gruff voiced man snapped.

Bella continued to try and free herself, in awe at the strength of the bindings and deducting that these people were too experienced with excellent techniques to be law enforcement. Panic rose in Bella like a river in flood as she tried once more to free her hands, *if they weren't law enforcement that means I am in way more trouble than I thought*, she concluded. She had managed to loosen the bindings bit by bit and she'd squeezed her hands until the knuckles on each index finger knuckle had dislocated with a satisfyingly quiet *pop!* Her hands then slipped through the rough rope binding with ease, swiftly she pulled the blindfold off and stood ready to fight, her eyes wildly searching the room whilst simultaneously adjusting to the dim light.

When her eyes had fully adjusted to the dank, dark room she saw that three men were sat in large ornate chairs, all three were wearing all black clothes with pieces of leather armour strapped on top in what looked like a ceremonial way. The man in the centre chair smiled which Bella thought was slightly creepy, given the circumstances. The other two men didn't move or looked particularly indifferent to her escaping their bindings.

"She's a keeper." He said to the other two men. This man wasn't one of the two voices the girl had heard earlier, but he was clearly in charge. She popped her knuckles back into place painfully, suppressing the urge to cry out. It was something she'd been forced to do many times before but she never got used to the pain, she forgot how much it hurt. She had been taught that move from a street rat going by the name of Slasher, in a city far, far away from where the girl was now, called Eyne, and it had saved her life on more than one occasion.

The man in the centre chair was grinning still, he looked at the men at each side in turn and then back at the girl.

"We would like to ask you some question s first,

before we tell you who we are, what we are." The man said, still grinning. The girl shook her head in despair, then tapped her throat with her index finger and shook her head again.

"Mute?" Said the man in the centre chair, leaning forward as if intrigued. The girl nodded her head and then mimed her hand holding an imaginary pen and writing on paper that was her other hand. The man nodded and produced a small notebook, a tiny ink bottle and a pen. The girl slowly walked towards the man, took the writing supplies from him and smiled her thanks. She then sat cross-legged on the floor in front of the men, refusing to use the chair that had been part of her brief imprisonment, close enough to show them the writing on the paper.

"Who are you?" Said the man with the gruff voice.

I don't know. She wrote.

"What's your name?" The second man said, tapping his fingers on the arm of the chair.

She wrote *Belladonna* next to the first answer as if daring to contradict it. Her handwriting was usually small so not to waste as much paper as it was an expensive thing to buy when you lived on the streets like she did, but it was beautiful; like she was trying to convey all her emotions through the beauty of her handiwork.

"What's your family name?" The gruff man barked.

I don't have one. Was all she wrote.

"Why is that?" The second man said. The man in the centre chair just watching, hand on his jaw, watching.

Because I don't have a family. Was crammed onto the same line as the previous answer, the truth on her face and in the small sigh she let escape once the men had read it, told the men that she was being genuine.

"How old are you Belladonna?" The gruff man said.

Fourteen? The girl wrote, shrugging her shoulders to show that she wasn't at all sure, she only thought that because that's what people had described her as whenever she walked anywhere alone. The rabid whispers of disgust directed at a girl so young for being unaccompanied.

"Perfect." Said the gruff man "A nice clean enrolment." Both men turned to the man in the centre chair and corroborated in a whisper.

"It appears we are all in agreement then," Said the man in the middle chair standing up, the girl stood up as he rose. Even though she had no idea why. "Welcome to the Assassins Guild, Belladonna." And shook her hand. She just stood there in silence, not just her silence, but the silence of the three men who seemed to make no noise, not even breathing; the silence of the building stunned her as well. It was as if everything was holding its breath, as if time itself had stopped, waiting for her to come out of her dazed state and return to the world, the ever-changing, ever-confusing world.

You're serious, aren't you? Penned the girl.

"Dead serious." Said the man, grinning.

What's your name? Belladonna asked.

"You can call me Charlie, but officially I am Charles the head of the Assassins Guild." Said Charles.

Bella smiled.

***

Two weeks had passed since Bella had begun her new life training with the Assassins guild. Since she was scouted in strange circumstances there was no one to vouch for her and be her mentor. So, Charlie, being the Head of the Assassins Guild took her to be his own prodigy, to other members' disbelief and outrage, he stuck by his decision even though in training the older initiates didn't take it easy on Belladonna. This only made her stronger.

Early one Tuesday morning it was time for the initiate sparring session, which was held in one of the Guilds main halls and was kitted out with mats that made it look like a temporary dojo. Belladonna hadn't been out of the Guilds premises since the day she was kidnapped, so she had no idea where it was, what it looked like on the outside or even how big it was on the inside. She also had her doubts that it was above ground, she had seen no windows so far in all the time she had been there, so they either liked their privacy in extreme measures or it was definitely underground.

Bella was scheduled to be sparring with Bobby, an older boy that had not only been there a lot longer than most of the other initiates, but his mentor was Charlie's rival in the Guild. Theodore Pascal. When Charlie gained the post of Head of the Guild he went up against some of the best assassins in the Guilds history, Theodore was one of them, and he had only become more relentless since his loss against Charlie all those years ago. And to make it even worse, the two had been initiates together and best friends. Putting the girl against Bobby was one of the ways he could get back at Charlie, because he so happened to oversee the initiates training schedule, and this time he wanted to win.

One of the key attributes that kept Belladonna alive on the streets for six (or so) years was the fact that she learned quickly, and she had a very sharp mind. What she didn't know was that she was to become one of the most successful Assassins the Guild, and the world had ever seen. Charlie saw this potential the moment he met her, which was why he became her mentor, he also knew that she would be strong enough to overcome the challenge brought to her by his own rivalry with Theodore.

"GO!" Shouted Theodore, a tall man with a handsome beard and a full head of greying black hair. It was rare that assassins live to such an experienced age, they never seemed to retire and even those who taught at the Guild were still working assassins.

Bobby lunged at the girl with his wooden sparring staff, she dodged it by leaning back sharply. Circling each other like wild animals, waiting for the other to make a move or open their defence. She struck out with the staff and connected heavily with the back of Bobby's right knee. He cried out in pain and dropped to his one good knee. While he was down she swung her staff again, this time aiming for his side, hoping to wind him. He blocked the attack at the last second lazily with his own staff, sending vibrating jarring down each staff and up into Bella's arms.

She backed away giving him enough time and space to get to his feet unopposed, she attacked again with both hands on the staff, purposefully hitting his staff causing them to form a cross, then she pushed with all her might against the cross, to little avail. The pair separated once more, Bobby tiring and Bella growing only more infuriated, she hit him again and again until she caught him off guard due to his lack of endurance, it was a weak blow in comparison to the earlier attacks but it was enough to send him spiralling away from her, flat on the ground with his own staff rolling pitifully away from him. She was about to finish him off with one great swing to the head when Theodore shouted the end of the match. If it had been the girl in Bobby's position, Theodore wouldn't have stopped till she was unconscious. She huffed at the injustice.

***

Sometime after the fight, during the initiates free time Bella sat, reading. This would all seem perfectly normal if she wasn't sat on one of the beams, high up in one of the greater halls. This was a place she liked to come, to listen, to escape. She always got secret information when she was sitting on her beam. It also meant Bobby and his trio of thugs couldn't find or even reach her. But Charlie could. A shadow fell across the pages of her book.

"Thought I would find you here." He said hopping onto an adjacent beam and sitting down, legs dangling freely in the open air below. She sighed, no matter where she hid Charlie would always find her and he would always appear unheard and unseen, like an Assassin should. He leaned over and pried the book from the girl's hands, turned it over a few times and then placed it on the beam in front of her, closed.

"Ready for our lesson today?" Charlie asked, almost rhetorically, knowing her thirst for knowledge. Especially if it was coming from the Head of the Assassins Guild, he seemed to know exactly what she wanted to know before she had time to even ask or even before she knew herself.

"Stand." He said, and was on his feet in seconds, stood stiffly but confidently on the beam. Obediently

Bella stood.

"Today Bella, *we* are going to be sparring." He said anticlimactically, as they spared every day without fail. He produced two wooden stave's half his own height, from god knows where and handed one to the girl. Who gave him a questioning look. "Up here." He finished. Her heart filled with a mix of fear and excitement, the resulting feeling was one of nausea. She nodded slowly and looked at the beams surrounding her. Like an unfinished floor, a derelict space almost. The gaps between the beams were monstrous, nearly a metre apart, one slip and she would plummet to the ground like a rock, although a rock might survive the fall. The ground being around thirty feet below, the ground being solid stone slabs. Bella imagined her own blood pooling between the cracks in the slabs, which not only reminded her of all the lives she had taken before entering the Guild, but it also strengthened her resolve, her need for vengeance that could only be sated by going through the Guild, surviving again.

If I fall I am dead.

If I fall I will never avenge my guardians or learn the truth about who I am.

…Then I better not fall.

Cautiously, Bella edged out further on the beam she was perched upon, gingerly at first like a dog being led over a rope bridge, then growing more confident with each step as her small feet weren't as wide as the thick wooden beams, meaning she wouldn't have to balance unpredictably on the edge like Charlie would have to with his large feet. The girl thought this might level the playing field a bit, but when she saw the way Charlie moved on the beams all those hopes were dashed. She moved slowly and cautiously on the beam like how a new-born deer looks as it takes its first steps, Charlie looked at home on the beam, twirling and leaping as if he had been doing it his whole life.

In one swift movement Charlie had crossed onto the beam where Belladonna stood, she gasped in shock and he laughed. She didn't know that he was that good, she had always assumed he was afraid of heights because he had never found her in some of her highest hiding places before. Oh, how she was wrong. She held her staff in a defensive position and planted her feet wide, so she would be less likely to be knocked over, a good plan since she didn't want to be a bloody splat on the floor anytime soon. Charlie lunged forward with his staff, perfectly balanced on the beam. Bella ducked and nearly lost her balance but steadied herself, ready for the next attack.

"I'm going to ask you something now and you don't need to answer. I'm not trying to put you off, I just want to know something." He said slowly circling around Belladonna, she listened intrigued at what he had to ask but also aware that contrary to what he said, that he might indeed be trying to put her off. She nodded.

"Your handwriting really is beautiful, you must have had a really good teacher, but you said you didn't have any family when we first met. And that you grew up on the street." He said almost questioningly, the girl just nodded.

"What I want to know, is who taught you to write like that?" He stopped circling and looked up from the beams.

Belladonna frowned at the painful memory of her guardians being taken away from her and that she was left to fend for herself, but then softened her expression as she remembered all the good times they'd all shared and the lessons they had taught her. She smiled at Charlie, then seized the opportunity and swung her staff at his knees. The staff connected with the back of his legs with a mighty crack and pitched him backwards into the gap between the beams. Into thin air.

For a second Bella panicked because she thought she had killed the Head of the Assassins, because he would never survive a fall like that, because he had disappeared. She finally mustered up the courage to look between the gap in the beams, to see no man shaped platter on the floor, no blood, no Charlie. She was relieved and confused, she looked around, to see him climbing up a rope attached to a grappling hook a few beams across.

"I must say," He wheezed almost breathlessly "That really did take me by surprise, not enough to kill me. But close. I think our lesson has been a perfect success, don't you?" He said smiling, she frowned at him, for making her worry and knowing that the smile he wore was because he knew she was concerned for him, like not many people have ever been. The smile was genuine.

They made their way back to the ground in silence, until Bella started scrawling on a small piece of paper. It said –

I was taught to read and write by some women who took me in when I was young, they were killed.

Charlie took the note, looked saddened for a second and then plucked the pen from her hand and wrote –

I am so sorry to hear that.

Those few words told Belladonna more about her

mentor than she had ever known before. The handwriting was neat, perfect in fact. Written with the same care and technique that she herself wrote with. She looked up from the page to question Charlie about it, but there were only the cold sad stones of the walls that surrounded her, harbouring more secrets than they cared to share. More secrets than she would ever know.

Who is Charlie really? Why doesn't anyone know his past? Why does the leader of the assassins have such perfect handwriting?

Strange questions filled the air around the girl and her notepad, she pushed them to the back of her mind as she set off towards the dining hall, hoping that a good meal would help her think better. She ripped off the page with Charlie's message on and tucked it inside the book she was reading, vowing to think about it properly later. She trudged off to the dining hall, stomach rumbling.

Chapter Five
The Truth

During her time at the Assassins guild Belladonna had undergone a series of different lessons and training programs and she had only been there for three months, the time in which she had honed her fighting skills and passed a series of exams, she was doing so well that she was put forward for extra lessons, Geography. This may not seem like a big deal but only three out of every set of initiates per year get put forward for this class and they are usually the ones that move through the ranks of the guild to take the highest positions once they graduate. This class was also brimming with classified information, since the world is mostly illiterate and uneducated, the things taught in the geography class had to stay a secret because as it's been proven, the truth is a bitter pill to swallow.

**

Belladonna sat in a small room she had never seen in her time at the guild, it was not only full of strange maps, news articles and lifelike drawings, it had two people she had never met before in it. Sat on her left was a boy, tall and skinny with bright, clever, sly brown eyes, blond hair and pale skin. She smiled at him.

"You're the mute, aren't you?" He said, not bitterly but with a sort of awe in his voice. She nodded.

"I'm Henry, we have training at different times, so I've never actually met you. But I've heard you're one hell of a fighter." Henry said beaming. Bella began writing and slid the paper over to Henry.

Thank you, Henry, I can tell we are going to get along just fine.

He read the note and smiled awkwardly, he relaxed a little after that leaning back into his chair and crossing one leather booted foot over the other at the ankle. The other student in the room was a girl, built like an ox and almost as quiet as one. She looked at Bella sternly when she smiled at her. Belladonna made a mental note not to get on the wrong side of that one and turned her attention away.

In the three months she had been at the Guild she hadn't made any friends, mainly because she was Charlie's only initiate whereas the other mentors had around ten initiates each, this meant she hadn't got around to meeting and communicating with many people, also probably because Bobby was always out to get her she didn't spend much time in communal areas, not that people would talk to her if she did. Many people couldn't read very well, and people always thought she was showing off because of her beautiful handwriting and the fact she was always top of the class. Always. Subconsciously she was also worried that anyone she grows to care for might leave her or die, like everyone else in her life up until this point.

The three of them sat behind the three desks facing what was probably the desk of the assassin teaching the class, there was a nameplate on the front of the desk that said Winters. *Winters,* she thought, *must be a coincidence...*She took the rest of the time while waiting for the teacher to look at the papers pinned to the walls. There were a lot of drawings that looked as if they were memories frozen onto paper, brilliant detail, of people that were wearing weird clothes, far too revealing for the current socio-political climate. Maps of places she had never seen before and drawings of buildings that could never be real, there just weren't the materials available that could make buildings such as the ones she saw on the walls. One particular picture was of a courtyard surrounded by immensely tall glass buildings, something that only a crazy person could possibly dream up because Belladonna thought there was no way that could be real.

Pain seared through her head unbearably, suddenly, she had never had a crippling headache like this before, she grabbed her head and closed her eyes, willing the pain to go away.

"Hey, are you okay?" Henry asked in a worried tone, leaning down to look at her and extending a long pale arm to touch her shoulder.

Belladonna's vision blurred, and it was as if all her senses had blacked out, as if she was no longer in control of her own body but she was still conscious, like a dream. When she was able to see again she didn't see the classroom, or her classmates. She saw people dressed in strange clothes, walking around in a place with strange buildings. Everything was too clean, too new, too different. Yet she felt like she belonged in this place, more than she had ever felt she belonged somewhere in her life, apart from the guild. There was a woman approaching her, this was when she realised she was on the floor. A clean floor with polished stone that looked almost new and well kept, unlike any she had seen before in her life. The woman looked concerned, the lines in her aging face wrinkling in an expression the girl could only guess was empathy, something no one had ever felt for her before. The woman had a kind face, with eyes like her own. *Is this a memory? Who was that woman? Where was I?*

Those were the questions that were circling in her head when her mind finally caught up with her body and blacked out. Back into the darkness.

***

Bella woke up in her room, to her it felt like only seconds after the memory but in reality, it was a few hours later when she finally resurfaced. Charlie was sat on the creaky wooden chair across the small dark room. He sat forward once he saw her eyes flutter open, and the chair made a loud creaking, which was what alerted the girl to his presence. He moved the chair to her bedside and smiled concernedly.

"How are you feeling?" He asked sceptically, whilst wincing slightly, like all bedside companions do when you have sustained an injury. Bella looked around for her notepad and scribbled.

I think I remembered something.

Charlie read the note and as he did deep worry lines wrinkled his aging forehead. Leaning back into the chair creakily, he sighed a deep, chest deflating sigh.

"I hoped this day wouldn't come, I could protect you while you didn't know the truth," He shook his head as he spoke, not making eye contact with her. His face furrowed with concern, "I took a risk with the geography class because you are our brightest initiate, I just assumed because of the extent of your memory loss that the class wouldn't trigger any memories. I would have alerted the wrong sort of people if I hadn't put you forward for the class given that you are the brightest initiate we have, the risk was too great, I am deeply sorry. I guess your mind is stronger than I thought, eh." He finally looked up and made eye contact with Bella, his deep brown eyes swimming slightly with emotion.

She sat up partly, and slid her notepad over to Charlie, a mixture of concern, pain and worry in her own deep grey eyes.

I need to know about my past, no matter how much danger it puts me in. I need to know. I have gone my whole life not knowing how or why I woke up one day memory-less and now I have the opportunity to know who I really am. Can you help me?

Charlie smiled, his resolve hardened once more, his eyes dry. He nodded.

"Before you graduate I promise you will know the whole truth, not just the Geography class truth but your truth. About how and why you are here. And how and why the guardians of your youth were taken from you. About whom you really are." He said sternly and inspiringly. Belladonna smiled triumphantly at first and then realised some important detail, she wrote quickly but surely.

I never told you about my guardians, I never told anyone about them. How do you know?

Not taken by surprise at this answer Charlie smiled a sly smile.

"I am the leader of the Guild of Assassins, I know everything." He said with a wink, and with that he left the room, in his stead a book. Not a very thick volume, but well-read as could be seen from the tattered leather binding and grease marks of people's fingers from over the years. It was titled, *History of the Earth: The Apocalypse,* and underneath had the numbers *2029 – 2043 AD & 0 – 36 AA.* The girl frowned, she knew that AD was '*anno domini*' and meant the year of our lord but she had no idea what AA meant.

With the intent of starting the book as soon as

physically possible the girl hid it inside her tatty mattress so that no one would find it before she had the chance to read it. She was still tired from the day's events and the memory had left her drained of all her energy, she decided she would begin the book as soon as she woke up. And with that, Belladonna fell asleep, dreaming of foreign buildings and weird people with strange clothes.

***

When Bella awoke, the sounds outside her door suggested that it was morning and people were on their way to their different lessons and going about their different lives. This reminded Bella that she had lessons first thing too, that she couldn't afford to miss anymore because she didn't want to look weak in front of the other initiates. She looked across at the one piece of paper pinned to her wall, it was a note from Charlie about the potions class, but she could barely read it in the dim candlelight. She groaned and sat up, potions class was this morning, and she was going to be late if she didn't hurry up.

She dressed in her usual clothes, stereotypically going against the gender specific clothes of regular society as the Guild usually did, she wore snug black trousers with bits of leather for added protection, a plain black tunic tucked into her trousers and knee-high black boots. The Guild didn't like women wearing dresses during training because they wouldn't be able to perform as well, although they would have to wear them in the field because they couldn't risk blowing their cover, this meant they had adapted to fighting in dresses over the course of their initiation. This was one of the many occasions when girls had to work harder than boys in training, one of the only times they weren't treated as equals, like outside the Guild.

She pulled her long thick black hair into a ponytail, splashed some cold water on her face and then proceeded to brush her teeth. Once she was ready she grabbed her notepad and pen and stuck them in the waistband of her trousers. Yawning, she left her room and joined the procession of initiates heading towards the lower floors, where the lessons were held.

She was just walking along trying not to get too beaten up by the flow of people when Henry muscled his way to her side.

"Hey, I saw you from down the corridor and I thought I'd see how you were doing, you did kind of pass out. The healer said you were just exhausted." He chatted excitedly. Bella rolled her eyes and wrote on her pad, which was difficult with several elbows all competing to knock her hand. The note was scribbly but still readable.

I'm fine, I just needed a good sleep. How was the lesson? Did I miss much?

"Oh, of course you wouldn't know, the class was cancelled. Charles said they wouldn't teach the lesson with only two thirds of the class there, it wasn't *viable*." He said sadly, then added "That other girl wasn't happy though, I'd stay away from her for a while if I were you. Anyway, got to dash, see you around." Belladonna sighed, she had never met anyone so intensely chatty in her life. She was glad for it, though, she had never really made many friends her own age and Henry seemed to be full of lots of important information and gossip, she was going to keep him close. It was always good to have a gossip on your side.

***

The potions class was in one of the larger rooms, nearly the deepest in the whole guild, they said that this was, so they could have the peace and quiet they needed but everyone knew that it was because if anything went wrong then only the lower levels would be destroyed and everyone would be safely evacuated to the higher floors.

When Bella arrived at the dungeon, almost all of her class of initiates were sitting patiently for the rest of the class to arrive, with bored and annoyed looks on their faces. This class was taught by the third guild-master Bella had met on her very first day at the guild, the chatty man that sat next to Charlie when they decided they would enrol the girl into the guild. He looked different to the first time she saw him, this time wearing normal everyday assassin clothes and not the special Guild-Master's robes worn at ceremonies and such events. He smiled when he saw her walk in, she sat down in an empty seat next to a boy with black hair that she had never seen before but looked like he wasn't likely to cause her any trouble or be too annoying. Her gut instinct about people was usually right.

Whilst waiting for the other initiates to arrive, the chatty man began distributing equipment; pestle and mortars, vials, knifes, cauldrons and other strange looking things Belladonna had never seen before she'd joined the guild and some things she had only seen when she worked part time for a cook in Donnol. She took this time as well to look around the dungeon, at the thick wooden work tables with deep cut fire pits in them, the scorched black colour that surrounded them

45

due to years of use, the occasional chunk missing where something had clearly gone very, very wrong. The room stunk of history; and that made Belladonna slightly uneasy, she'd always had the strangest feeling history wasn't all it was cracked up to be.

"Okay listen up," The chatty man boomed, the room fell silent immediately "My name is Griff and I am one of the three Guild-Masters of this Assassins guild, so you better do exactly as I say, or I'll clout thee round the head, got it?" He asked rhetorically knowing that, that one line always worked, every year, without fail.

Bobby sniggered from across the room. All eyes in the room turned to look at him, the fiercest were those that belonged to Griff.

"Something funny, boy?" Griff boomed, staring menacingly at Bobby. This made the boy sit bolt upright, suddenly paying attention.

"Oh n-nothing." He said scrunching a piece of paper quietly in his hand, struggling to maintain eye contact with Griff. Griff strode over to Bobby in a matter of steps, which would have easily taken a smaller man twice as long. As quick as a viper he grabbed the boy's wrist, which crunched slightly under the pressure, Bobby winced and let out a pathetic noise, one not dissimilar to a small dog being kicked. Griff leant close to the boy's face and whispered something so menacing only Bobby would be able to hear it. Bobby dropped the paper and went as white as a ghost.

"Read it." Griff whispered louder, drawing himself back up to full height and cocking his head to one side as he crossed his arms across his wide chest and stared at the boy. Bobby trembled at the sight of the huge man towering above him. After what seemed like forever he broke eye contact with Griff and looked down at the note, clearly regretting that he had been caught.

"Maybe there's a potion that will …" Bobby said quietly, murmuring the last part so people at Bella's side of the room wouldn't be able to hear it. Several people looked over at her with looks of fear and disgust in their eyes. She sat more upright in her seat, craning to see Bobby, her heart pounding menacingly in her chest.

"LOUDER!" Griff roared right in the boy's face. Trembling Bobby looked over at Bella and then back to the paper in front of him.

"Maybe there's a potion that will make the mute speak." He said, suddenly ashamed and held his hand up as a gesture of his sorry-ness. Bella went from mortifyingly embarrassed to angry in a split second, it was like her heart had stopped beating altogether, she grabbed the knife from the workbench in front of her and launched it at Bobby from across the room without thinking. Even Griff didn't have time to react or even anticipate her move. The whole class just sat astonished, mouths agape, still looking at her seconds after her knife had hit its mark. Her mark being Bobby's outstretched hand, his writing hand, his sword hand, the hand he had held up in false apology. Blood was gushing down his arm and onto the cold stone slabs of the dungeon floor long before he registered what had happened.

Griff didn't move to help him or to punish Bella, he just looked at Bobby calmly and nodded to the door. At this prompt Bobby sniffled in both upset and anger, trying not to cry in front of his classmates he clutched his shaking, bleeding hand around the knife that was now lodged there, and left the room. Noticing the class was still staring at Bella in either awe or fear, Griff walked to his worktop, rearranged some bottles absentmindedly as though thinking of the right words to say and then spoke.

"Today we are going to be making a deadly poison, designed to subdue a mark to weaken them before death. A form of liquified hemlock designed for arrow tips or to slip into the drink of a target, because of the latter it means the poison is extremely difficult to get right. The slightest mistake and the hemlock is ruined, got it?" Griff said cleverly to get the class' attention. All eyes were suddenly back on him, Belladonna sighed in relief. She had managed to calm down somewhat by the time the black-haired boy looked over to her, he didn't look scared or shocked he just smiled. When he smiled, it wasn't just with his mouth, it was somehow also with his eyes, the first genuine smile she had seen in too long which made her give a weak smile in return. They both looked back at Griff, and that was it, all he wanted was a smile, to know that she was okay. And then she was.

"Your instructions are on the blackboard, ingredients are at the front and I trust you're all mature enough to choose your own partners. You have one hour. It's in your best interests to get this right, so if you need me I'll be at the front." Griff said as a matter-of-factly as he could manage. "Oh and *we will* test the potions at the end of the class, anyone that fails to concoct anything short of a *perfect* poison will stay behind at the end and scrub all the cauldrons clean. They will also have to write me an essay on the importance of correctly brewing poisons in relation to carrying out their contracts." He said the latter with a smile on his face, he knew well enough that the initiates had enough to be getting on with without having to make up for a shoddy potion.

Planning on working on her own, the girl got up and collected the necessary ingredients from the front table and returned to see the black-haired boy hadn't moved, in fact he was furiously scribbling down the instructions written on the board, unaware of the bustle of activity around him.

Bella had plenty of experience creating potions with her guardians (although they had been the healing kind, the good kind) and had spent a good portion of her time working in kitchens as she travelled across the country. People were always keen to hire her, she could act sweet and innocent when she wanted to and once they saw her expertise with a knife they hired her almost immediately. She reminisced for a while, whilst she created a small fire in the pit with ease and began chopping ingredients carefully, she stopped when she realised she was being watched. It was the black-haired boy, who looked apologetically at her.

"There is an even number of initiates now, do you mind if I work with you?" He said, shrugging his gangly shoulders so high he appeared to have no neck. Bella scowled in thought for a second and then thought it might not be such a bad idea, she nodded. He nodded in return and began measuring some of the liquid ingredients and pouring them into the cauldron, which began slowly sizzling and bubbling turning from green to yellow to red as each new liquid mixed itself into the cauldron. The boy looked back over at Bella and finally spoke again.

"My name is William, but you can call me Will, if

you like." He said, his deep brown eyes looking familiarly sincere. His outstretched hand tanned and strong looking.

Nice to meet you Will, I'm Belladonna but you can call me Bella, if you like.

She pushed the note to the black-haired boy. She took his hand and shook it once. He smiled and continued to stir the cauldron.

Soon all the ingredients were in the cauldron and all that was left to do was to carefully wash all the equipment they had used and slowly stir the cauldron while maintaining a medium heat, like the instructions had explicitly said. A burning smell circled around the room coming from the Ox and her partners cauldron, Bella tried not to look at the burnt, misshapen spoon the Ox pulled out of her cauldron, covered in a gooey black liquid, she also tried not to look at the scared look on the Ox's partner's face as the Ox threw the spoon at her, smothering black oozy liquid on the girl's face.

"YOU IDIOT." The Ox screamed, her voice echoing around the room. Her partner screamed out in pain as the apparently corrosive liquid burned her skin. The Ox's face was crimson with anger and shaking with rage. *Yep, don't want to get on the wrong side of her, she will never make a good assassin with a temper like that,* Bella thought. Speaking of anger, she hadn't known where her own short burst of anger had come from earlier and she hoped it wouldn't impair her ability to become a great assassin.

"Go to the infirmary, Eloise. And you, clean this up." Griff barked at the pair.

"Another one bites the dust." Whispered Will quietly to Bella, watching Eloise leaving the room, covering the blistering on her face with her pale, shaking hands.

Finally, all the potions were ready, one hour after the ordeal with Bobby. Griff came around each pair with a fresh toad, with criteria unknown to the initiates he decided that had the best potion was Bella's and Will's, not to anyone's surprise, because Bella was the top of the initiate class, it still made people sigh with envy and irritation. Bella and Wills toad had died immediately after coming into contact with the poison and looked as though it had just decided to take a nap, Griff must have thought this to be superior to some of the other initiates toads' deaths. Bella thought for a second that she better watch her step if she wants to make it through initiation without being slipped one of these potions, then she smiled to herself, making her look like a psychopath, which would also hopefully keep people away from her, if they were clever. Glaring eyes from the handful of initiates that had to stay behind to scrub the cauldrons followed Bella and Will, they left the room feeling pleased with themselves.

***

Belladonna had sparring after potions so she walked back to her room to drop off her books and change into something more appropriate. When she got back to her room she saw a note had been slid under the door while she was out, she picked it up and read.

Geography has been rearranged for the same time next week, try and keep your emotions in check next time - Charlie.

She frowned at the note for a second then crumpled it up and threw it towards the bin in the corner of the room. *Keep my emotions in check, what the hell does that mean?* She shook her head and put it down to Charlie being stressed, he did have a whole guild to run after all.

She changed quickly and fell into step with the other initiates on their ways to lessons. A shape barged it's way to her side.

"Hey!" Said Will, "I was thinking, since we bossed it in potions and you kind of took out your sparring partner that maybe… you could spar with me instead?" Belladonna looked shocked and shook her head, she didn't want to hurt him. They didn't rank initiates in the guild but everyone knew who was the best and who they could easily beat, Will was below Bobby, the Ox and Bella in the running for top spot.

"You won't hurt me, don't worry." He said smiling, "And I won't hold back this time, time to show everyone what I'm really made of." He laughed and hurried away before she could give him anything in response. *What does that mean, not hold back?* Bella hurried after him towards the training hall.

Once in the training hall the assassin supervising the training paired everyone off and since Bobby and Eloise weren't fit to fight it changed up the pairings slightly. Bella had thought this would foil Will's plan and she would be put with the Ox but when the pairings were announced her stomach sank, she was with Will. How he had managed to fix that she had no idea.

"Well, well, well." Said Will as they reached their designated mat. Bella frowned at him and shook her head.

"Let's see what you got." He said smiling. They faced each other on the large mat and bowed, they were taught to do this as a sign of respect to the opposition but it wasn't always the case in more tense matches. Bella was barely out of her bow when Will came lurching towards her, fist retracted, ready to strike. Bella was surprised but she dodged, sending them both off balance. She righted herself and sent a kick straight into his ribs, he wasn't quick enough to move out of the way, he gasped and clutched his ribs. Bella's expression softened for a second, she really didn't want to hurt Will, it was one of the things that made Bobby such a good sparring partner. She hated him. She barely had chance to finish that thought before Will threw a kick of his own, with a breathy gasp of pain from the ache in his ribs. His foot caught Bella behind the knee and she staggered, long enough for Will to come back again with a punch aimed straight for Bella's jaw, something that would likely knock her out. Instead she flattened herself to the mat, bending back on her knee to avoid the strike. This threw Will off balance and he pitched forward, following his own fist. He landed directly on top of Bella. For a split second it looked like he was going to say something, his expression softened and a smile crept onto his lips. Bella felt heat rising to her cheeks, was she blushing? Despite her feelings towards Will, she didn't want to seem weak in front of their class so she made the most of his hesitation and landed a punch squarely on his jaw with her right hand, the hand that wasn't being pinned to the ground. He was out cold and rolled off her like a ragdoll, Bella stood up to straighten her clothes and saw the whole of the class staring back at her. Was it because of the blush that they were staring at her or the fact she had knocked him out? She couldn't tell. The supervising assassin came over to her and patted her on the back.

"We have a clear winner over here, the rest of you need to step your game up." He said. "Belladonna, you may go. The afternoon is yours." He added, staring at the heap of clothes of the floor that was Will. Bella smiled a false smile at him and strode out of the hall without looking back.

Chapter Six
The Outside

Belladonna hadn't been outside in months, she had been stuck inside, training, learning and worrying that she was letting her guard down because she was getting too comfy, too sheltered. After reading a bit of the book that Charlie had given her, she decided that she would have to go outside, becoming too used to the safety of the guild wasn't good for her. She had spent too many years being on her toes, always wary, never staying in one place too long in case she got too attached to the people there, in case they died. Like Hazel, Maple and Juniper.

The worries began not long after the girl had arrived at the guild, when she began having flashbacks of her life on the outside, as if her mind was trying to make her feel guilty for feeling comfortable, for feeling safe. One night, after potions class, after she had shown the guild the type of person she had been before, the type of instincts she had and the way she used to deal with people who dared to cross her. This was a tactic she had adopted just to keep her street credit high, so that people wouldn't mess with her, so she never had to feel weak again, never abused again. This was the reason she had reacted the way she had in the class earlier in the day, she needed to establish a reputation as someone that shouldn't be messed with to survive.

The worst flashback came on that night, when she was exhausted from the day's events and she had finally passed out on her small lumpy bed in her small room at the Guild.

Exhausted due to her long journey, a small girl with long black hair and pale skin like that of a porcelain doll collapsed under the rough wool blanket her guardians had given her, with her bag clutched tightly in her hands. She had stopped in a wood, just a few miles away from a village, she thought it would be safer if she arrived there in the morning, and anyway, people scared her. She didn't want to have to sleep with one eye open because of all the thieves and murderers of villages.

So, she slept in a pile of autumn leaves dropped by the large oak that kept her sheltered from the wind and the rain. But the oak could not keep her safe from the people. A horse drawn cart ambled through the night, towards the village, towards her. Two men sat at the front of the cart with several women and children sat behind. In what would have seemed like a coach for hire, the women and children sat, some sleeping, some weeping. This was no coach for hire, this was a slaver's cart and these people had been ripped from their homes, from their families and marched through the night off to some foreign land they had never dared ventured to.

Belladonna wasn't visible from the road to the normal eye, but the slavers were hawkeyed, money grabbing, people snatching creatures that could spot a needle in a haystack if it would fetch them the right price. There she lay, finally ready to begin her new life in this new village, finally ready to trust people again after what had happened a few months previously to her guardians.

The slavers slowed their cart, and one of them jumped down. There were two men, one was scruffy with only a couple of yellow teeth left in his crooked mouth and was wearing a scruffy and obviously stolen cloak, it was one of those things you could see was of the highest quality and clearly made for the higher classes but had been worn so much it had its own unique look about it. The second man, the one that had jumped down from the cart was the complete opposite, he was clean with a kempt beard and his curly brown hair looked like he washed it often, he was wearing a simple white tunic, that was white, the whitest she thought she would ever see.

He walked over to the small lump under the tree and knelt next to it. He placed a hand on Belladonna's shoulder and gently shook her awake, which didn't take long because she was constantly on edge. She gasped when she saw the man, she took in his appearance and calmed slightly, but she couldn't shake the feeling that she had seen this man before.

"Hello." The man said, his voice was soft, and she could already tell that he was highborn. She tapped her throat and shook her head, even in the dim light from the moon the man could tell what she meant. He seemed to think for a second before he spoke.

"Ah a mute. I know the perfect home for you sweetheart, come with me and I'll take you to live with a dear friend of mine?" He asked, his soft eyes dancing in the moonlight, his outstretched hand looked like it had never done a day of manual labour in its life. Everything about him was too trustworthy, but she wanted to trust again. She also thought that she would never get this opportunity again, and a girl of her age shouldn't be wandering the streets alone she convinced herself. So, she went with the man. Why did she go with the man that fateful day? Whatever made her trust him? Why was he so kind to her?

Belladonna gathered her things and went with the man, they walked through the woods for a short while, the man put one hand in his mouth and whistled a long high-pitched whistle just after they had set off. Then they made it to the road.

"Why are you all alone, little girl?" The man said sadly, knowing she wouldn't reply to him "No one should ever be alone in this world." He continued sadly looking up at the shining stars only visible occasionally, through the hazy atmosphere.

They walked in silence the rest of the way to the village, occasionally slowing so the girl could catch her breath because the man had a very quick stride, it was both insistent and lazy at the same time. When they had reached the village, they walked to the high street, a ghost street of empty shops and lives due to the darkness that once scared the girl so much, they took a left after passing a bustling tavern onto a wide alley. When their footsteps on the cobbles had become the only sound, the man stopped. He turned to the little girl plodding by his side and sighed sadly. He knelt and squeezed her shoulders, smiling encouragingly.

"This is the house of a Lady Catherine, this is the backdoor because it would be rude to call on the front door at this time of night. She will look after you and teach you how to be a proper lady, you will do just fine here if you just do as she says okay little one?" He said instructively and friendly.

Belladonna nodded, scared and excited at the same time. The man nodded in return, stood up and then knocked on the door. The knocks seemed to boom all through the alley, the only sound in the deepest of night.

A man answered the door. He was a short, thin man that stood bolt upright wearing his penguin suit. He looked down his hooked nose at the man then down at the scraggy little girl on his mistress's doorstep.

"Ah Winters, what can I do for you?" He said, almost spitefully.

"I wish to see Lady Catherine, I have a present for her." The man, referred to as Winters said cheekily, as if he was winding up the penguin man. The man frowned and then retreated into the building, leaving the door open so that the two of them could follow him. They stepped into the building. What Belladonna thought from the outside was nothing compared to what was inside, there were lush sofas making a waiting area, in front of a grand staircase that was trimmed with gold. Lady Catherine must have had a very rich family, Bella thought.

Just as they had sat down an elegant Lady wearing a long crimson dress, that was just a little too revealing for her age, with

58

its back cut with a deep V all the way down to the small of her back.

Bella stood up immediately and tried to remember everything she was taught about how to act in front of a lady, she curtsied when the woman came close. This made the woman emit a loud screeching noise that normally would never pass for a laugh, but she was a lady, so.

"Oh Winters, she is positively delightful!" Cooed Lady Catherine inspecting Belladonna closely. "I'm going to call this one Cecile." The man in the penguin suit gasped, earning him a hard, sharp and sudden slap from Catherine. He just bowed in return and left the room.

"Cecile was the name of my dear late sister, Jefferson has been in my family since I was just a girl, he must have seen the resemblance. He must have." Catherine had gone from angry to sad in a split second, Winters patted her on the arm for comfort, this was what brought her out of her sudden trance. She stood straight, smiled falsely and then grabbed the girl by her arm.

"Come on Cecile, I'll show you your room." Catherine dragged the girl away, her bony fingers digging into the Belladonna's arm so painfully she would have cried out if she could have.

"Lady Catherine." Winters called over to the Lady as she approached the foot of the stairs.

"Yes Winters, Jefferson will handle your payment, now leave." Catherine said offhandedly, not even turning to look at him for she was too busy with her new toy.

"No Lady Catherine that's not what I meant, the girl… she's a mute." Winters said. The woman stopped suddenly, then looked down at the girl beaming an insane smile. Belladonna just looked back at Winters with betrayal written so clearly on her face that he had to look away as she was dragged away up the stairs and out of sight.

"Here, Cecile, here's your room." Catherine said as she

pushed the girl through a doorway into… a shrine. Well it wasn't really a shrine, but it looked the same as the day the real Cecile had departed it, bed neatly made, chest of toys ajar, dresses strewn across the back of a comfy chair near the window. Bella was disgusted, and it showed on her face. As if determined to wipe the look off the girl's face, Catherine slapped the girl so hard she was thrown to the ground silently sobbing, clutching her burning face with one hand and clutching her bag of worldly possessions in the other, sobbing. Sobbing.

Sobbing was how she woke up. Coated in sweat and tears, Bella sat bolt upright, tears still streaming down her face. Anger filled her, anger at the tears that fell. She ripped the covers off her and strode to the door, pounded it once with her fist and then slumped to the floor, head in hands, tears no longer falling. She vowed she would never cry like that again, that she would never feel the way Catherine's abuse made her feel. That she would never be that weak again.

That was when she decided. *Is this place making me weak? How long can I stay cooped up in here? I need to get out.*

That was when she decided she had to get out. She wore the long black winter cloak, designed for when they let them out of the Guild to train, so it would cover her trousers. Women on the outside only wore dresses that were socially acceptable. For some unknown reason the Guild worked differently.

She grabbed her throwing knives, she had stored them under the floorboards just in case and put them through her belt. They felt comfortable in the place they had always been, she no longer felt as naked, as vulnerable as she did when without them. She looked once again around the room and sighed, how could this place have made her feel so safe when now it only made her feel trapped and frustrated. She never wanted to feel weak again, she wanted to be strong enough to help other people like she needed to be helped all those years ago, that's why she had come around to the idea of becoming an Assassin because they usually only killed the scum of the earth and she felt like scrubbing the scum from the earth was a good enough calling for her.

She headed for the door and threw up her hood so no one could see her face and then all she did was walk straight out of the front door. She had scoped out the top floors before tonight just in case, she needed to know her exit if she was trapped underground for the rest of her life, so she knew exactly where she was going, and she just had to look like she belonged there.

There were two guards posted next to the two heavy ornate wooden doors, mainly to stop people coming in rather than from leaving but they were always suspicious of any initiates that came close to the doors. They didn't know it was her because she was dressed for the field, so she managed to just slip straight past them, it was too easy, she headed down the street, scaled the side of the Blacksmith's empty workshop without anyone seeing her and laid on the roof looking at the entrance to the guild with suspicion of her own.

Nothing out of the ordinary happened in the half an hour she waited on the roof. She frowned. There was no way Charlie would know she had left but she had the strangest feeling she was being watched, like all the times he had sneaked up on her in the past. She shrugged, climbed down from the roof and threw down her hood, her long black hair scraped into a ponytail cascaded down her back.

She walked for hours, practising being unseen by

the people on the streets, which was a lot of fun and was tonnes easier than practising sneaking about in the Guild full of assassins that could hear you coming a mile off. She shadowed a woman who was on her way to the market stalls laden with various groceries, to buy some delicacies for the people she works for no doubt, she had no idea she was being watched by the figure in black, the figure that clung to the shadows and the edges of the world.

She continued to tail people, stalking them in the constantly ebbing and flowing throng of people in the village, forcing the flashback out of her mind and all concerns about the Guild with it by making up stories in her head about who they were and where they were going.

Bella finally decided to return to the Guild after a few more hours, she snuck in through the front door the same way she left and down the corridors to her room. She didn't believe she had gotten away with it, the adrenaline coursing through her veins made her feel almost happy with what she had been doing the last few hours, but she knew it was too good to be true because when she returned to her room she saw a figure sat lazily in the chair beside her bed. Charlie? It was too dark to see for sure; all the adrenaline now made her feel guilty at the disappointment she knew he would feel at her absence.

The figure didn't say anything, it was only until she lit the candle by the door that she realised it wasn't Charlie at all, it was another man, a sleeping man. Immediately wary, the girl pulled a dagger from the inside of her boot and quietly crossed the room.

A floorboard creaked as she reached him, and the man jerked awake, fearful at waking in the unknown.

Bella closed the distance quickly and held the blade against the soft flesh of his neck.

"Stop! Please, I'll explain why I'm here just remove the knife." He glanced up at the girl riskily, pleading with his eyes. "…please." He begged. She removed the knife from his throat and stood in front of him brandishing the knife jauntily.

Go on then her expression said.

"You don't know me, but I am a friend. You are a part of the Geography programme, aren't you?" He asked, knowing that was the exact thing that would raise an interest in the girl. He was a fairly tall man with a tatty beard and shoulder-length curly brown hair, he looked like he'd had a hard life and was probably younger than he seemed.

She nodded.

"I am a part of the Guild, a Historian, a Geographer. I've come here tonight to tell you the truth, you are the most promising initiate we have had in years, since Charles in fact. But Charles has changed, he is not as head strong as he used to be. You…" He wagged his finger at the girl excitedly "You however, you can save us all. You can change everything! But you must promise me that what I tell you tonight will not make you leave the Guild, you must wait till after you graduate before you embark on the path this information will set you upon. Promise?" His eyes were desperate, fearful. The Historian looked tired, beaten almost but when he looked at her his eyes were so full of desperate hope, nearly masking the fear. He must have been the same age as Charlie but looked much older, probably because the Historian was cooped up in the guild the whole time whereas Charlie had to remain fit, young and agile or else he would have been dead for years like all the other Guild masters before him and those before him. He was the youngest and longest lasting Guild Master the Guild has seen in decades after all.

After a short silence Bella nodded. *What was he going to tell me? Will this change anything? Is this what I'm meant to do?*

The aged historian sighed a sigh of relief and smiled, beckoned for her to take a seat on the bed and then opened a large book that had been sitting on the floor for the whole meeting.

"Listen carefully, what I am about to tell you has not been told to anyone that hasn't graduated the Guild and even then, not everyone knows, else the whole world will have been upturned already by now, thrust into chaos. Which is why I am telling you. You will have the tact, I hope, to tackle the problem at the source and not by invoking the masses in tumultuous chaos.

OK, it all began in the year 2029 after years of abuse to the planet, earth had finally given up, it wanted rid of the parasites that crawled on its surface. Scientists at the time hadn't predicted the end of the world for at least another hundred years so they had no idea how to deal with the event. So, Bella, the world ended in 2029. How, you wonder?

A worldwide Volcanic Winter, imagine a volcano, a super volcano with the power to erupt over 1000 times bigger and more violent than a normal volcano. This Super-volcano was located under Lake Toba in Sumatra, Indonesia. It caused enough ash and dust to rise into the atmosphere and cloak the earth, stopping all light rays from reaching our surface, increasing the earth's albedo. This increased the reflection of solar radiation on the planet's surface. You are probably confused as to what this means, it means that the global temperature dropped, a lack of sunlight, storms and flooding due to abnormal rainfall. A volcanic winter. This was a recipe for famine. Are you following?" He lifted his head up from his book to see Bella looking pale, her face drawn.

Bella nodded glumly. He nodded solemnly in return.

"The global famine and natural disasters lasted for a decade, whittling the human population down to around one million from the eight and a half billion recorded in the year 2029 before the eruption. That's the geography of it." He sat up and closed his book, laying it careful on the bedside table next to him. Bella's head was reeling. *Volcanic winter? Apocalypse? If the world ended, why are we here now?*

She turned to the man scowling intently; she reached for her pen and began scribbling determinedly. She shoved the finished product over to the man, who had to squint to read the paper in the little light of the girls' dark chamber.

I understand that the world ended in 2029 through the means of famine and natural disasters caused by a Super-volcano, if that is true then how come we are here now talking about it. I've seen pictures of a world that doesn't exist, seen buildings that can't be real.

"You are a very intelligent young lady that's for sure. That is why you need to be the one to change our future. Mankind survived accidentally, and those survivors are being manipulated by The Castle, the hub of our new world, the place where all the decisions are made in this seemingly lawless and decrepit world. The world as we knew it ended in 2029 but our story didn't, would you like me to tell you why? To tell you the role I would have you fill? Or shall we save that for another night? It is late, and your brain has had a lot of information already tonight." The man said, he did look exhausted, the girl thought. *I want to know more, I want to know how, I want to know everything.*

The girl's thirst for knowledge was evident in the disappointment she showed when the man stood up and took his book with him to the door.

"Same time, tomorrow night. My name is Declan Winters. Come see me anytime, my office is at the back of the archive room in the lowest level of the guild." He nodded his farewell, but the girl grabbed his arm. *Winters.* He didn't look like the Winters she had once known all those years ago.

Winters? She scribbled.

"Yes, that is my name. What's wrong?" He said inquisitively.

I knew a man called Winters once, he sold me as a slave when I was a young girl.

Thought passed over the man's face, then a scowl. "I am so sorry to hear that Belladonna, I know the man you speak of, but he is not I. That is a story for another night I am afraid." And with that Declan Winters left her chamber and the girl was alone with her thoughts once more. *Who is this man? How does he know so much? Why is he telling me?*

Bella sat on the chair next to her small bed and began to turn over all the information the man had given her in her head, it did make sense, that she had to admit. There was nothing left for the girl to do but to finish the book that Charlie had given to her, she would have been more clued up on what Declan was saying if she had only focused her time on reading the book instead of parading around outside the Guild.

By the time she had finished reading the book it was light and the sounds of the bustling Guild made her realise how tired she was. She was told to act normally until she met Declan again, but she had been reading about it all night and she had so much to ask him, so many theories as to what he needed her for. She decided to continue her day as normal, she had gone without sleep for longer than this and she wouldn't be able to sleep anyways, her mind was too active.

She started the new day by going to the canteen for breakfast, she tidied her hair and splashed some water on her face and then set out. She made some toast and poured herself some orange juice and sat at a long wooden table in the corner of the hall, alone. She wasn't alone for long however as she was soon approached by a figure. She grabbed a knife from the table and swung around at the shadow behind her, to her surprise, the boy caught her arm and smiled his genuine grin, eyes laughing.

"Nearly got me there, Bells." Will said, taking a seat next to her. Belladonna smiled an apologetic smile in return. A nickname? She'd never been given a nickname before, and that was the beginning of the greatest friendship she had ever experienced, so far in her short life.

"Don't worry I get it; it could have been one of Bobby's goons. But we all know you don't need a knife to take me down, do you?" He said between mouthfuls of porridge. The girl thought about asking him why he was sitting with her, especially after publicly humiliating him in training, but she stopped herself. At the time she didn't know why she let the boy so close, after everything that happened to her in the past she knew that it wasn't a good idea. She didn't want to lose anyone else but there was just something about this boy that intrigued her more than anyone else she had ever met.

So, they sat in silence for a while until the boy had finished his porridge.

"Hey, next time you sneak out of the Guild can you let me know in advance? I'd like to accompany you." Will said off handily. So that's who was watching her that day, she thought she felt Charlie's presence, but it was Will. That's when it hit her. She started scribbling.

You are Charlie's kid, aren't you? And I don't need to be accompanied anywhere, thank you very much. I can handle myself.

The boy grinned the biggest grin she had ever seen, and that is when she saw Charlie in him. The smile. The presence. He bent his head close to hers and lowered his eyes.

"Yes, but it's a pretty big secret. I don't know how you worked it out, I haven't given anything away. My father was right about you though, you're *very* clever. The Guild doesn't know anything about who I really am, and it could lead to my father's death if they found out. So, I trust you to keep our secret." Whispered the boy. It was a stab in the dark, but Bella had known enough people in her short time to have grown incredibly intuitive. She almost couldn't believe it.

"Aww young love, the mute and the loner!" Boomed a voice from across the canteen. Bella stood up immediately to face the sound and stood defensively. Will stood by her side and shouted back.

"If you think you're too far away for her knife to reach you Bobby then you will have a hole in your other hand as well." He spat the words with such force that Bella couldn't help but smile, making the pair seem more menacing. Thinking he was at a safe distance Bobby laughed, followed by the echoing laughs of his goons. Bella picked up the knife off the table and launched it across the room, seeming to miss all the bystanders and lodging itself in the wall right in front of Bobby's laughing face. The knife was still wobbling by the time Bobby had left the canteen, the girl had never seen him move so fast before. Silently laughing Bella sat back down and resumed eating her toast, she could feel the ecstatic energy coming off Will as he took his seat next to her.

"So earlier when you didn't stab me, you could have? It wasn't that I was faster than you at all?" He enquired. Bella shook her head heartily, smiling.

"Nice throw." He replied, trying to remain calm from the excitement of the altercation with Bobby. *That boy just doesn't learn does he*, she thought, irritated at all the public scenes he was causing.

The pair had sparring again that morning and made their way to the training hall soon after the incident with Bobby.

When they got there Theodore was standing in the doorway.

"Belladonna, a word." He said abruptly, gesturing for Will to enter the hall alone. Bella nodded, more to Will than to Theo. When the two were alone Theodore took her aside away from earshot of the hall door.

"It is my understanding that the duel between Bobby and yourself has caused a … rivalry. Charles and I have been speaking and this needs to come to an end, the only way to do that is an elimination duel. When Bobby recovers from his … injuries. We made the decision last night." He shot her a spiteful look. "Because of this you and Bobby will not take part in the group training sessions anymore but will have personal tutoring from now until the event. An eliminating duel is as you can imagine a very serious Guild procedure and tradition, the elimination aspect will be, how can I word this delicately. Death. We have not made this decision lightly but as it looks like one of you will kill the other anyway, we have decided to make it on our own terms, a fair fight." He genuinely looked like he meant every word of what he was saying to the girl. That was when from nowhere Charlie and Griff appeared.

"I will take it from here Theo." Griff boomed, shaking hands with the smaller man and entering the training hall. Charlie smiled a sad smile at Belladonna and shook hands with Theo, who left abruptly after.

Charlie sighed.

"I didn't want it to come to this Bella, after what's been happening recently, we could come to no better conclusion. I have every faith in you, but just to be on the safe side I wanted to train you myself. As did Theo with Bobby."

He took her to one of the smaller training halls, one she had never been to before and for good reason, this one was lined with weapons. Swords, knives, bows, maces, battle axes, spears, even the occasional dawn star. It took a second for everything to sink in, the girl knew that she had to win this fight, it wasn't only her life on the line. Declan Winters was relying on her to carry out a mission for him and for that she ideally needed to survive until that point in time.

Her eyes grew wider as she began to take in everything in the room in more detail, there were no sparring weapons here at all.

"Preferred weapon of choice?" He asked, admiring a beautifully ornate sword.

Knives, but a sword will probably be better.

Charlie laughed and handed her a light rapier with impeccable balance, she smiled. She once knew a guy who fought beautifully with a rapier, but his was no match for this specimen. She was taught how to sword fight on the streets, so she was probably not up to the standard Charlie wanted her to be. She couldn't believe that this was happening, being made an example of in front of the whole Guild, *I bet they do this every year to keep all initiates in line*, she thought bitterly.

He picked up a broadsword and swung at her heavily, she parried sloppily and spiralled out trying to regain balance after his heavy blow. She swung blindly while regaining her balance to try and put him off, he wasn't holding back this time like he had done in all their training sessions ever before. He hit her again and again and again until she couldn't bare it anymore, she had never come up against a foe like him, someone so coordinated, strong and agile unlike all the street rats and gang members she had fought before.

They parried, slashed and dodged until Bella was exhausted. Charlie insisted on continuing until she was battered and bruised, he himself had remained mostly untouched by Bella's blade and seemed as though he could carry on for hours. She had a long way to go before she felt like she could not only risk her place at the Guild but her own life as well. Her clothes were torn, and she was bloody even though he had tried to only hit her with the flat of his blade to minimise damage. Otherwise she wouldn't have lived to fight Bobby.

"Good we can stop for now, that was impressive however you need to improve vastly. You will be taken out of all your afternoon lessons for the next few weeks leading up to the trail to prepare." He said almost dejectedly, then he looked back up at the exhausted battered girl and smiled "Go get something to eat and then sleep, I will see you tomorrow for round two." The girl forced a smile in reply and put the rapier back onto the rack where it belonged and left the hall. Once she'd exited through the heavy wooden door (which was much heavier than usual after their training session) she realised that they must have been training for longer than she had originally thought. The corridors that were usually bustling with activity were now empty, this immediately put her on edge as she realised that this would be the perfect time for someone to attack her. She was somewhat vulnerable after the intense training session and she was alone in a place that was full of trained killers. Which until today she thought would be the safest place anyone could be.

She walked the usual hallways until she got to her small bed chamber in the east wing of the student dormitories, encountering no one. Nothing was out of the ordinary when she entered her room, on the first initial viewing. When she looked around a second time there was a small note just in the doorway, like it had been pushed under the door in a hurry. She crossed the room back to the door and picked up the note, which was written haphazardly. It was from Declan Winters.

Bella,

It is with a heavy heart that I must write this note, I'm afraid that time has caught up with me and I cannot help you further in your quest for the truth, I have been informed that there will be a Guild wide search in the near future. They will find me, and they will kill me, so I have fled.

You are probably wondering who I am on about, The Castle. They are the source of all this trauma, for me and for you, they will hold the secrets that you wish to uncover about your life and about everything you have ever questioned in your short time on this earth. Please forgive me, I am a coward, I was hoping to run into you to tell you in person, but fate hasn't seen it fit. Burn this note when you have read it because no one can ever know that I was here, the secrets I have shared with you will put you in danger. Also try to be scarce when the search happens because I believe they will be looking for you too, you are an asset for us and they will want you dead. When this all blows over I will try to contact you again, if I live. Don't trust anyone. Be careful. Don't let your guard down and DO NOT leave the Guild's premises.

Declan Winters

P.S - the "Winters" you are looking for will be a part of the search party for The Castle.

She burned the note.

Chapter Seven
Sssssh this is a Library

In the days following the strange note, the reality of the upcoming trial was beginning to seep in. Bella decided to set her mind to learning everything she could, mainly to try and get back to normal but also secretly hoping she could learn something that would give her the edge over Bobby.

She roamed the halls of the guild, running her fingertips along the rough stone walls as she walked. Her light footsteps were all that could be heard. She often did this at night when the halls were silent, she liked the openness of the maze like corridors. It made her feel, strangely, less trapped. She had always hated being cooped up in small spaces or rooms for too long, she liked the open air, she liked to be able to escape.

"The guards don't like people wandering around the corridors at night, you know." A voice said from the shadowy crevice of an upcoming doorway. Bella hadn't been surprised to find someone else stalking the halls in the middle of the night, it was calming if the guards didn't catch you.

"I was sure I'd scare you this time." Will said and flashed a smile, his brilliant white teeth were almost luminous in the dim light. Bella smirked, he never scared her and each time he tried she became less and less scared of him. Day by day her guard was slipping, for the first time and she hadn't even realised it.

"So I have a fun idea." He said, falling into step beside Bella, who hadn't stopped walking or even slowed to acknowledge his sudden appearance. She looked over to him and raised her eyebrows inquisitively. "It's long been an initiate tradition to break into the library to try and steal *Mors Grimoire,* the most sought after book in the whole of the guild. It's literally Deaths' book of spells!" His excitement made his voice break and like all boys his age resulted in immediate embarrassment, something they couldn't teach you to avoid in the guild. Bella looked over at him and sniggered, watching him blush an ever deeper shade of red. She punched his shoulder jovially and nodded. They were going to break into the library. She felt a rush of excitement, her heart beating that little bit faster than normal, she skipped almost silently the rest of the way down the corridor with Will jogging to keep up with her.

***

It had been close to midnight by the time the two teenagers had ironed out all the flaws in their plan to break into the library and steal the *Mors Grimoire.* They were going to do it that very night before they lost their nerve. They sat opposite each other with their legs crossed, studying a hand drawn map of the guild. Will looked up into Bella's deep grey eyes, candle light dancing across his face playfully and he began to speak, she watched the shadows play across his face as she hung onto every word he uttered.

"This has only ever been done twice and scores of initiates try it every year. The first to do it were three young initiates, no-one can agree on the actual details of that night because everyone told it differently, but it was epic.

It all started when the book was scheduled to be moved to a large library in the Castle, word got around that it was because the Castle had failed to corrupt and destroy the Assassins guild so they were going to try and limit their power instead. The Guild Master at the time had agreed to hand over the book in exchange for all guild activities being absolved. There was a huge ceremony in which the King and the Guild Master co-signed a law absolving all guild activities in front of hundreds of people from all over the country.

Whilst this elaborate ceremony was happening the initiates crept into the library vault where all the rarest of books are kept and drugged the guards. Using a non-lethal poison obviously as three of the eight guards were assassins. They stole the book and hid it. The King was furious at the Guild Master, who knew nothing of this crime. The King demanded the Guild Master and everyone present in the guild take a truth serum to find out what had happened to the book.

This would have been a brilliant idea but you'll never guess what? The initiates, had brewed and taken a potion that negated the effects of the truth serum, a potion that no-one in the known world had ever been able to come up with. The initiate that invented this potion had been keeping its existence a secret since he invented it, so only the three of them knew of it. It was the perfect plan. When it came for the three initiates to take the truth serum, they were able to lie to the King. The whole guild and surrounding village had been forced to give their alibi's for the ceremony but not a trace of the book could be found." Will's voice was in a whisper by the end, revelling in the art of storytelling. Bella had been enveloped in the mystery and sheer brilliance of the tale and hadn't noticed how uncomfortable the floor was..

They were still sat cross legged on the floor of her

chamber, floor plans of the guild spread out in front of them, steaming cups of herbal tea sat untouched by their sides.

"Any idea who they were? The initiates." He sat back all matter-of-factly trying to conceal the smirk on his face. Suddenly the spell was broken and Bella sat back, brow furrowed as she was deep in thought. She had read about the guild's history but she had never come across a story like this before and there had been no mention of a visit from the King in any of the records, so she assumed Will had been told this story by his father.

She never would have been able to guess if he hadn't given it away at the last second. She scribbled three names on a piece of paper and handed it to the ginning black haired boy opposite her. His face dropped as he read her answer.

"What! H.. How did you guess?" He blurted, looking from Bella to the paper several times so quickly Bella thought he must have made himself dizzy. She scribbled again.

The way you told that story, you only ever speak like that when you're talking about Charlie. Griff is the best potions master the world has ever seen, I read that somewhere, I think or maybe he just told me he was. As for the third person, I know Theo and Charlie were best friends when they were initiates, so logically that was my third guess.

"Yeah I don't have as good a poker face as you do Bells, good detective work. I'm thinking maybe you chose the wrong profession." He said getting to his feet and stretching, his body stiff from being sat on the floor for too long. "Ready for the heist?" He said excitedly.

Bella stood up and cracked her back, knees and

knuckles in a way that had always grossed out Will. Bella always relished the look on his face when she did it. Once she was done she began to nod but something stopped her, she picked up her pen and notepad and began to write rapidly.

That was the first time that the Mors Grimoire *had been stolen by initiates but when was the second?*

Will pondered over the note for a second and stifling a smirk said "Tonight." Bella nodded her head and smiled, showing a full set of pearly whites. Will had seen her smile like this on many occasions in the time that he had known her, but most people that met her could say that they had never seen her teeth before and would probably be scared if she smiled.

They gathered their supplies and made their way to the door, not needing to psych themselves up because of the overpowering level of adrenaline shooting through their bodies. Bella had nothing to lose if they were caught as she was already facing the guilds judicial system for her behaviour but she was worried about Will, she wasn't sure he'd be able to get away with what they had planned. They slipped out of their boots and socks and left them by the door.

"Ready" Will whispered, he stood so close she could feel his warm breath on the top of her head. She nodded. She pulled the balaclava over her head, which was almost unnecessary due to the colour and volume of her hair. They were both wearing skin tight black clothes head to ankle, each had a specially made leather bracelet loaded with six flat metal vials (something Will had invented himself) filled with various trouble making concoctions they had brewed in Bella's washing basin just hours before.

They felt like they were read y for anything, Bella

had even made sure Will had a pocket full of sand just in case. This, she explained, was to throw in the eyes of an assailant so they couldn't identify you, or even to get the upper hand in a fight, it was a dirty street tactic she'd picked up in the south. She never left home without her trusty pocket full of sand.

They slipped out into the corridor and navigated the maze that was the guild, they had timed their heist between the movements of the guards, information they had both unconsciously picked up from their nights wanderings. They moved like shadows along the empty halls, silently. Going painstakingly unnoticed, they reached an empty classroom twenty meters away from the library.

They exchanged a furtive glance once they were sure they hadn't been seen entering the room. Will raised his balaclava and took a deep breath…

***

Giggling and ecstatic with adrenaline, the two teenagers stumbled into Bella's chamber, the thick black leatherbound book clenched tightly in Wills arms.

"We did it! Gosh, once that guard wakes up he is going to be pissed." He beamed, pushing his dense messy black hair off his face. "Right, I'm going to sneak back to my room in case they do a sweep. You hide that, okay? Good job Bells." He tucked the balaclava into his trouser pocket and grabbed his boots on his way to the door. She watched him leave, watched him glance back as he closed the door quietly, flashing one of his signature smiles that never failed to make her involuntarily smile.

Her heart was racing. Was it because they had just stolen the most sought after book in the guild? Was it because they would go down in guild history? Was it because of Will? Or was it because she had to hide the book that everyone would be looking for? They had planned to hide it for a few days and then once the story had spread through the guild and everyone was talking about it, they would casually bring it up in potions class to Griff and watch everyone's faces as they realised it was them who had pulled off the most daring heist of their generation.

She didn't hide the book right away, she reckoned that it would be a few hours before the guards woke up and realised what was missing, at least. She sat facing the door on the floor of her chamber surrounded by books and notepads in case anyone walked in she would be able to hide the book amongst the others and explain that she was studying for the trial. She read by candlelight until dawn, copying the more interesting chapters into her little black notebook. Smiling the whole time.

***

It went down exactly as they had expected it too, Griff was beaming with pride as he sent them to the Guild Masters office, something that was no doubt to be seen as a punishment. They walked the corridors with the book stowed under Bella's arm comfortably. Will kept glancing sideways at her to see what she was thinking but she caught him looking every time and all she could do was smile. Bella wondered as she looked up into his face, whether he was scared or whether his nervous smile was to do with the fact they had pulled off the second most elaborate heist the Guild had ever seen.

They reached the door to Charlie's office and looked at each other as if daring the other to knock, Will caved first and rapped on the heavy wooden door. They stepped back and a voice from the other side boomed "ENTER!"

The nervous smile had dropped from Will's face and was replaced with something Bella couldn't quite work out before he pushed hard on the door to reveal Charlie sitting prominently behind his heavy set desk. Bella took a deep breath and followed Will into the room, half wishing she wasn't the one holding the stolen book.

Chapter Eight
An Amphitheatre of Chaos

In the weeks leading up to the trial by combat, Belladonna was ruthlessly pushing herself to the physical and mental extremes, for herself, for Declan, for the truth. Declan had disappeared three weeks ago with no sign of either him or a raiding party on the Guild. Bella began to wonder whether he was telling the truth about any of it or if he was just your run of the mill coward, scared about what he'd told her.

She'd continued her training for the trail every single day with Charlie and that had been taking up all her brain power and hours, so she had very little time to think about what she was going to do after the trail, especially since she didn't know whether she was going to survive it. *No point making plans if you aren't going to live to execute them*, she thought. With this in mind she had been attending her lessons but keeping everyone, she had previously been engaging with at an arm's length, Will and Henry mainly. There was the occasional person who would come up to her and wish her luck for the trail as they wanted her opponent to die horrifically, which gave her hope because she was starting to feel sorry for the bully she was going to kill. The Guild was making her weak she thought to herself more than once a day, although her training said the opposite, she was the strongest, quickest and the most skilled she had ever been.

Bella was making her way towards the training halls when she stumbled upon a very heated, hushed conversation. She stopped in her tracks and listened carefully to the voices that sounded like they were coming from around the corner of the corridor.

"... We can't allow her to live, she is too dangerous. You are aware we set this up to be rid of her! You said we couldn't possibly fail!" A stranger's voice spat.

"No Gus, you cannot interfere with matters like this. It's official Guild matters now, we cannot do anything about it, we *won't* do anything about it." Hissed Theo's voice in return. This barely surprised the girl, of course Theo wanted her dead, but who was this stranger to intervene in the trail of the Guild? She had angered many people in her short lifetime, but none bore the name Gus and none in the Guild who wanted her dead as much as he seemed to.

"You *must!* She cannot live to find out the truth, it will change everything!" Gus hissed desperately. She heard the dejected sigh of Theo and footsteps leading quickly off into the distance. As far as she could tell it was only one man's footsteps, which would mean the other was still blocking her way to the training halls.

Bella stood in the hallway for a little while longer and thought about the conversation that she had just overheard, she wondered whether she should risk having a look at the man that wanted her dead but decided that it would be too dangerous, especially since the man had clearly put some measures in place to ensure her death. *What was the truth? Why do they want to keep it from me so badly? Who the hell is Gus?*

She walked to Charlies office instead of the training hall because she knew that if she didn't find him soon it would begin to look like something was wrong. She let herself into the large chamber of the Guild Masters Office and sat down lazily in front of the regal looking wooden desk placed in the centre of the room, that was otherwise filled with bookshelves. She was reminded of the last time she had stepped foot in this office and hoped that this time Charlie would not be as mad. He was impressed at their heist, no doubt, the part he was mad about was Will drawing attention to himself. He had been disappointed that Will had been willing to risk both their lives and Charlie's own status in the guild to impress a girl. Charlie was equally as disappointed in Bella as he had assumed she'd worked out Will's identity, that she didn't show more loyalty towards him in the face of everything he was doing to ensure her own survival. It was brutal. They had both left the office feeling sick with guilt, only to be reminded every two steps of it by initiates patting them on the back and congratulating them on pulling off the heist of a lifetime and telling them they'd instantly become legends in the guild.

She sat for about twenty minutes before Charlie came back to his office, he saw her sat there and looked puzzled.

"Well it's a good job I came to get my coat before going out to look for you then wasn't it." He said in a jokey manner, but she knew he wasn't joking. Bella handed him a long note in which she had written all about the reason she hadn't gone to training and about the strange meeting with Declan Winters and what he prophesied would come to pass. He stood in silence for a while after reading the note.

"These men, do you think that they are the same person?" He asked finally, his hand on his chin.

She thought about it for a second and then replied…

It's possible, I didn't see the face of the man talking to Theodore in the corridor.

"Okay, well I have never heard of a Gus here at the

84

Guild, and I'm the Head of the bloody thing! I don't know who he is or what he wants but I'm glad he has gone. You need to be more careful..." He went on ranting at the mute girl, she just sat in the chair and listened, drawing a spider diagram of all the recent events. She realised he had stopped ranting, it was then she looked up at her mentor, who was looking at her diagram with interest. She wrote a note separately...

Something doesn't add up here, if I am in as much danger as you say I am, then I need to know all the facts and I need to know them now.

She slid the note over the regal looking table to Charlie, who looked as though he had just solved the puzzle all by himself. His eyes wide with shock. The girl rose slowly from her seat, looking from her mentor to the diagram. On the diagram were loosely written notes about; Declan Winters, Gus, the trial, venturing outside and ... Will. All the things she had experienced at the Guild that had either come as a shock to her or didn't quite add up.

"Do you think you can win against Bobby?" He was all serious now, all traces of the jokey mentor had gone and in its place was the stern look of a trained killer. Bella thought about it for a while and then scribbled on her pad once more.

If the fight isn't rigged then yes absolutely, but I have a suspicion that it's not going to be a fair fight. He looked up from the pad and she saw that he matched her suspicion, he sighed.

"The fight is tomorrow, go get some rest and I'll send someone I trust to guard the door." He said almost dejectedly, "And one more thing, try and stay out of trouble until the fight please." With that, he let her leave the room and walk the long way to the dormitories, alone. She opened the door to her chambers carefully, looking for any signs of a trap or someone hiding in the darkness, but found nothing. *How boring*, she thought. Bella sat on her bed, head reeling with the events of the past few weeks that would all come to one big finale tomorrow, she was worried, she didn't doubt her own ability one bit, but she did doubt that the fight would go un-sabotaged. She thought back to Charlie's comment about not getting into any trouble before the morning, which was less than eight hours away, and thought *Oh ye of little trust*. Suddenly there was a knock at the door which sent her brain into overdrive, she spun around and took the knife out of her boot, just in case.

"Hello! Bells, it's me Will, can I come in?" Said a voice behind the door. She relaxed immediately and walked over to the door, opened it roughly and stared menacingly at the boy behind it, raising her eyebrows as if to say *Well what do you want?*

"What a warm welcome." He said brushing past her and into her small bedchamber, she closed the door behind him. Found her pad and wrote…

Charlie sent you *to guard me?*

"Yep you better believe it. Think about it, it does make sense." He said taking the chair and facing it towards the door, he looked up to find Bella just looking puzzled at him, *how could that make sense*, she thought, *usually a guard is more skilled than the person they are guarding.* "A big burly guard waiting outside your room would tip off any potential saboteurs that you were on to them, but a boy sneaking into a girl's room the night before she may potentially be killed, they are going to think nothing of that now are they." He smirked flirtatiously. He pulled two long knives out of his boots and laid them across his lap as he sat down in the chair.

Charming. Was all she wrote. He just smiled cockily in return. She ignored the boy and got into bed.

"Also, good luck tomorrow. I don't want you to get brutally killed in front of everyone we know, okay?" Said Will, completely serious now. She nodded at him sincerely, she didn't want to get brutally killed in front of everyone they knew either.

Bella closed her eyes and darkness came for her again, just like it always did.

***

Meanwhile, Charlie was sat at his desk staring at the mind map of events Bella had left there earlier that day. He didn't know that Declan had been corresponding with her and he certainly wasn't happy about it. Their agreement had been that Charlie would allow Declan refuge at the Guild as long as he posed as a Historian, someone who wouldn't be seen by the majority of the Guild. Charlie put his head in his hands and sighed, racking his brains, *how had Bella pieced together almost everything that he knew himself?* She'd linked the Castle to the apocalypse and knew their role in the sedation of the general population to quell uprising, she knew they were keeping everyone away from the dread zone on purpose and that they were keeping everyone uneducated and poverty stricken so they had little time to stew on conspiracy theories. *She must have read half the library archives,* he thought. The only thing she hadn't figured out yet was her involvement in the whole thing. He sighed again, a deep heaving breath. He thought he would have longer to get the story right before telling her but it looked like he was going to have to tell her sooner than he thought. *She's too young for this responsibility,* he thought, *if only we could have tracked down her sister instead, she was older and had a more credible claim.*

The only thing he hadn't banked on was the return of some of her memories, they had all believed that the memory serum that had been used on her was too powerful with her being so young at the time. It made him wonder if the damage on her ability to talk would be affected by this, but he pushed the thought away. *No use dwelling on if's, she doesn't need to talk for what we have planned for her, she just needs to be seen.*

It had taken him years to find her and she'd barely been at the Guild a year and he was already struggling to keep a grasp on her, keep her safe. He thought back to the day he saw his mother's cottage burning, how his Aunt Maple had told him with her dying breaths that he had to find the girl, told him who she was, how important she was. He'd been beginning to think he'd never find her, it had been nearly eight years but he never stopped looking, people were beginning to wonder why he spent so much of his time outside the Guild. Then she came stumbling right into his grasp! Just in time too, the Castle had been hot on her trail and she was kicking up a stink looking for his mother and Aunts. He'd heard on the grapevine afterwards that Castle loyalists had sent word they'd spotted her in the town but lucky for him, he'd got to her first. *What would they have done to her if they'd got there first?* He shuddered at the thought.

Chapter Nine
Trial by Combat

Bella woke early the next day to find Will sat in the chair opposite the door, fast asleep. *What a good guard dog he was*, she thought. She watched him sleep peacefully for a couple of minutes, his chest falling and rising gently, his black hair flopped lazily against his forehead, hands tightly gripping the knives on his lap. She ran to get a thick leather-bound notepad and began scribbling in it frantically for about fifteen minutes straight, once she had finished she shook her hand and grimaced. Semi happy with her work, she got up quietly and dropped the heavy book Charlie had lent her on the floor at Will's feet, he sat bolt upright, knives brandished menacingly. Bella laughed silently, Will looked around for a second in shock and wonderment until he realised she was messing with him.

"Sorry I fell asleep, was there really any need for that rude awakening?" He grumbled as he put his knives back into his boots and stood up from the chair, stretched and made for the door. Bella grabbed his arm and gestures for him to wait. She handed Will the leather-bound notebook with a note attached. Eager to know what was so important he began reading aloud from the attached note, but the girl stopped him and he then understood that it wasn't the time. He put the book in his pocket and opened the door.

"Do you want me to walk with you to the canteen?" He asked glumly. She nodded and then gestured to the pile of clothes on the footstool. "Ah yes of course, get ready and I'll be waiting in the corridor." He left. Bella sat down on the bed and sighed, she had wished to tell her life story one day in more detail, with more time. But there was no more time, the fight was at midday. She got ready in silence. Wearing her best black leather trousers (by that she meant the ones with no holes in already) and her baggiest tunic, she hoped that if she wore a baggy shirt then Bobby wouldn't know exactly where her body was inside it. Small victories. She washed in a basin of cold water next to her bed, immediately regretting not getting any hot water but kind of glad for the refreshing awakening and brushed her teeth for what might be the last time. She put on her knee length boots, this time without the knives hidden there, just because she was worried someone else might cheat, she wasn't going to. A move that might cost her, her life, but she had been ready to die every day for the past eight years, what's a couple more hours? She went to open her door, but Will got there first and pushed his way inside. She scowled at him.

"I know you told me not to read it yet, I only had a peak, but I was so confident that you would win today that I hadn't even thought of what I would do if you didn't and you writing this made me doubt myself, what if I never said goodbye properly? I wouldn't forgive myself." He was looking at his feet whilst talking to her, which she thought was uncharacteristically strange for Will. He looked up at her, mind made up, suddenly calm and collected.

He kissed her. Bella had never had any time in her, *fifteen?* years for romance, she had been forced to defend herself from drunk men throwing themselves at the young beauty, but she had never had any feelings of her own. She kissed him back, her hand against his chest ready to push him away. She pushed everyone away before situations like this had time to happen. His hands crept into her midnight hair and they kissed passionately for what seemed like forever. They broke apart naturally, her hand still resting on his chest and smiled at each other, both simultaneously ecstatic and sad, they then headed down to the canteen. Her mind was spinning. She hoped he wasn't trying to put her off the fight, he wouldn't do that surely, it was just bad timing. She pushed all thoughts of Will and the letter she'd wrote to one side and ate breakfast in silence next to Will thinking only of the fight. A few people milled around the canteen waiting eagerly for the fight to start, some came and patted her on the back or wished her good luck, she smiled her thanks and shook hands with a few fellow initiates, teachers and assassins that had turned up for the big event. Initiates fighting to the death was a once in a lifetime event and assassins from all over the world had turned up to witness it themselves. People whispered as she walked past, on her way to the training hall to meet Charlie for one last session before the fight. She left Will at the door, she kissed him on the cheek softly because she forgot her notepad and she had no words that she deemed appropriate now. He smiled and squeezed her hand.

"Good luck, you'll kill it!" He said ironically as he sauntered to the stands to watch the much-anticipated fight. She rolled her eyes and opened the door to see Charlie wearing his official robes, *no sparring today then*, she thought.

"Ah you're here, early, good. I just want to wish you the best of luck today, there's going to be a lot of people watching but don't let that put you off, don't let anything put you off. I have brought in unbiased referees to make sure everything is fair and legal. There should be no surprises, if all goes to plan. If anything should happen, I'm sure you will make the best judgement call. Now. Meditate, clear your mind." Charlie said quickly but firmly, confident in every word, they sat on the matts in the hall and closed their eyes like they had done many times before during training. Mediation, focus. She tried to push everything out of her mind; Winters, Will, that kiss, the history book, everything but the fight. She opened her eyes and saw Charlie staring around the room, not meditating.

"You think I'm going to sit here with my eyes closed just before a fight like this? Hell, no, someone could have killed us both here and now and it would be over with before it even started. I wanted to give you the best chance at winning today. Ready?" He said calmly. Belladonna nodded. She *was* ready. They made their way to the Great hall where the fight was to take place, he stopped her when they reached the huge wooden doors.

"Belladonna, good luck, remember your training." Said Charlie smiling sadly, he pulled her in for a hug. It was the kind of hug that made you feel at home and at peace with the world, a comforting fatherly hug that made you feel like everything was going to be okay. She hoped that everything would be okay. They broke apart and he pushed her ahead of him through the large doors into what sounded like pure chaos.

They made their way to the grand hall where the seating stands had been erected for the fight, they could hear the audience cheering and murmuring before they even got to the door. An amphitheatre of chaos. The audience erupted when she entered the hall and made her way to the ring in the centre.

She waved and smiled, searching in the crowds for one face, one face that would ground her. She was pushed into the fighting ring, faces whirred around her, the noise was petrifying. She took deep breaths and focused herself on the one person she needed to focus on, Bobby was being ushered into the ring at the other side of the room. Two referees came in with him and stood in the centre of the ring, they beckoned to the audience for quiet, silence echoed around the hall immediately.

"Right, Guild rules state the following: no poison, no other weapons, silence from the crowds, all other tactics and rules apply. It's a fight to the death, do you both understand?" Boomed the senior referee, his voice filling every space, every ear and rafter in the hall. The girl nodded, Bobby nodded as well. She still searched for Will in the crowd but couldn't see him, she found Charlie and Henry beaming down at her and that made her feel a little bit better. The second referee wheeled out a large stand full of weapons of all kinds. "These have been kept in my care all night and have not been tampered with, if we find that they have been then the consequence will be execution as the rules dictate. Are we clear?" Nods all around again. "Then we may begin. Chambers, would you search the lady and I will search the man." The referee named Chambers was female, even if she didn't look particularly feminine. She walked over to the girl and began patting her sleeves, body and boots.

"Clear." She said, returning to the older man in the centre of the room.

"Clear." Said the senior referee from across the

ring.

"Choose your weapons carefully as we will not allow you to switch them throughout the fight, under no circumstances. Choose!" Bella walked to the rack of weapons, knowing exactly what she was looking for, it was a shame Bobby knew exactly what he was looking for as well and it didn't bode well for her weapon of choice, he went for the mace. A big heavy weapon for a big heavy boy, Bobby was at least 6 ft 4 inches with blond wavy hair, he was built like a blacksmith. He wasn't a clever boy, that's what Bella was hoping would give her the advantage, after all it was what got them into trouble in the first place. He could easily pin her down and bludgeon her to death with that mace, what she needed was a weapon with a longer reach and a speed advantage, knives wouldn't be enough to sate the crowd and they didn't have throwing knives, so she would have to get close but she didn't want to go anywhere near that mace. She opted for a rapier like the one she had practised with in training, it had the reach, it was light, and she knew how to use it. She weighed it up in her hands carefully, now able to fully ignore the audience shouts and heckles.

She turned back to the referee with the weapon she had chosen, a determined look on her face. She looked for Will again with a fresh set of eyes, a focus she had been learning from Charlie in the months she had been at the Guild but still couldn't find him. *Where was he? Was he just a distraction after all? Was he telling the truth?*

She pushed all those questions from her mind as she took her eyes off the crowd and onto Bobby, the referee and that damn mace.

"Silence! SILENCE!" Screamed the senior referee to the audience "I must insist on silence from now until the end of the fight, the fight is to the death. There will be no further consequences for the winner of the fight, as the matter will be settled, take care to remember that when your favourite dies! On my whistle the fight will begin. Ready?" He said the last part to the two fighters, they nodded one last time and prepared themselves for the possibility that they may be the one to be killed.

Bella looked around once more and fixed her gaze onto Charlie, she smiled one last time at her mentor to show him that everything was going to be alright, that she had accepted her fate.

Twoooooooooooooooooooooooot!

The piercing sound of that whistle rang out and was the only sound to be heard in the whole Great hall. Bobby swung immediately trying to catch Bella by surprise, she dodged backwards anticipating his attack. She balanced the sword in her hand carefully and then swung it menacingly around from hand to hand, trying to put Bobby off, trying to scare him.

He ran at her, she didn't react straight away, instead she waited till he was nearly upon her before slashing at him while he thought he had the upper hand. He put up his left arm to take the blow. Sacrificing his weaker arm to the flesh slicing bite of Bella's rapier, it took a second for Bobby to realise what had happened, after a painstaking moment the gash opened and started pouring thick crimson liquid all over the Great halls stone slab floors. She looked at his shocked face and smiled, *he had no idea what he had gotten himself into when he joined this Guild*, she thought.

"Bitch!" He spat, blood gushing onto the ground, the wet splashing sound as it hit the ground was the only sound to be heard in the whole hall. He charged at her again, mace ready to bludgeon her to death, his face pale, his eyes bloodshot like a rabid animal. She danced around him, trying to tire him out, it was a good tactic because so far none of Bobby's attacks had hit their mark.

Bobby stopped suddenly and vomited, Bella came up behind him with the intent of putting him out of his misery, she wasn't going to toy with him anymore, she placed the point of her blade under his left shoulder blade and took a deep breath. He realised what was going on as soon as he felt the point dig into his back, the whole hall went quiet, it was deafening. Not defeated yet Bobby swung his mace straight back and into her shin, there was a sharp snapping sound, a deep grunt from Bobby as he put all his energy into the attack hoping it would be enough to save his life. Bella slipped in the nauseating mix of blood and vomit and landed hard on the ground, winding herself. She gasped, the pain in the leg was like nothing she had experienced before, sharp and throbbing. How could she possibly win now with a broken leg? She scrabbled to reach the rapier which had been thrust out of her hand as she fell, she reached, fingers almost stretching out of their sockets. *This is what I get for trying to make it a clean, merciful kill. Well not anymore, get ready Bobby,* she thought. Bobby, pale with blood loss and exhausted raised the mace again and came down towards Bella, towards the ground. She grasped her weapon in time, rolled over and attempted to block the attack, the sword shattered into a mosaic of tiny pieces, leaving only the hilt and a blade the size of one of Bella's throwing knives usable. She closed her eyes and rolled away, the blade had managed to deflect the shot a fraction to her left and as she rolled she missed the brunt of the attack, her shoulder barely being scraped by the mace.

Somewhere in the crowds stood Will, frozen with fear and anticipation for the last few seconds he decided to take out the note she had written for him.

Dear Will,

In case I die today I want you to read the enclosed book, it's a brief recollection of the events of my life in hopes that you can get to know me better after I am gone. You are the only person I have met that I feel I could ever have become really good friends with in this life. You might get to understand what that means later but for now just read. Tell your father that he did the best he could for me, which is more than anyone has recently, he's a good man. If I die, you can have my throwing knives, they are the only thing of any worth that I own, good luck.

Love, Belladonna.

He sighed, warm tears rolling down his cheeks, he looked up to see the author of the note laid mangled on the ground soaked in blood and vomit, most of which was not her own, in front of a crowd of people he now despised, fighting for her life.

Bobby was shocked at her attempt to deflect the blow, he was almost completely exhausted now, small fragments of the girl's blade had entered the skin in various places on his lower body. He dropped the mace, it was too heavy for him now and she was much quicker than he was. He had her pinned to the ground with his body.

"There's no chance you can win this now mute, you're dead." He spat in her face as he wrapped his thick fingers around her throat. Blood from his open wound trickling onto her face. "Any last words?" He mused and began to squeeze increasingly tighter. Bella looked around one last time trying to focus on finding Will. And there he was, shouting something she couldn't hear, then she remembered something. She pushed against Bobby's chest with her hand trying to free her trapped other arm and brought the pathetic remains of the sword up slowly, she could feel the cells in her body slowing, her vision began to falter as her body gave in to oxygen deprivation. As quickly and accurately as she could manage she jabbed the shattered blade into the side of her attackers' neck. And twisted. The twist wasn't necessary but he had really pissed her off and she wanted to make sure it hurt. Blood poured all over her like a fountain, the thick fingers loosened from around her neck and the heavy crushing weight of Bobby's lifeless body pressed her harder into the ground.

She closed her eyes. She had won.

Chapter Ten
An Unlikely Ally

Bella opened her eyes expecting to see the Great hall with its ancient wooden ceiling beams hanging above her, instead all she saw was darkness. She went to put her hand to her throbbing head but hit something else instead, something warm.

"Ssssshhhh! Don't move, don't make a sound until I say so okay? I'll be back soon. Don't move!" A voice whispered frantically into the darkness, a thin strip of light appeared not too far away, and she saw a silhouette slip through it, *ah a doorway*, she thought. So, she stayed, she didn't quite know why she listened to the voice, she didn't recognise it, in fact she thought she probably had a concussion from when she slipped in the blood and hit her head on the ground. She closed her eyes once more, she was exhausted. Her whole body ached, and her shin was still exploding with pain. *Guess I can't just walk this one off,* she thought to herself sarcastically.

"Wait here okay?" He said, she nodded and sat hunched down in the bottom of the wardrobe once more. "I'll come back for you, I promise." It was one of the servants from the kitchen that would hide her whenever Lady Catherine's guests would get too rowdy. He had always protected her, in all the months she had been with Lady Catherine he had been the only one who treated her properly. Lady Catherine treated her like a pet, something to drag out and show off to her guests, something to hit when she was upset, something she owned. Jefferson treated her like she wasn't even there sometimes, forgetting that she needed to eat and drink and hardly ever acknowledging her existence. But John was just fifteen, a serving boy in the kitchens, he protected

her like he had to protect his sisters from his drunken father at home.

Bella waited and waited and waited. Eventually she fell asleep.

"Cecile! CECILE! Where is she? Where is my Cecile?!" Catherine squawked about the large house in an enraged frenzy. Bella woke up to the sound of doors slamming and Catherine's piercing voice echoing down the corridor. She was too scared to move, too scared of what Catherine would do to her if she found her hiding in the wardrobe. She decided she would run away, she had been abused by the disgusting old harpy for long enough, her mind was racing. Where can I go? How do I escape? What happens if she finds me?

She sat in the bottom of the wardrobe panting, thoughts whirring around her head like a whirlpool. Bella opened the wardrobe door a slither, just enough to see into the servant quarters, she listened intently, her heart pounding in her ears, she looked around frantically. Had she waited long enough? She clutched her small bag of belongings to her chest and slipped out of the old rickety wardrobe and onto the splintery floor, barefoot. She was wearing a beautiful old dress that used to belong to the Cecile, the real Cecile, it was burgundy with carefully stitched navy-blue flowers. It made her nauseous to even think about the clothes that she was made to wear, about how sick it was that Catherine was dressing a mute orphaned girl in the clothes of her dead sister.

Bella slipped out of the wardrobe and into the cold room, she took a deep breath of crisp cold air and tossed the bag around her shoulders, ready to run, to escape, to live her own life. She tiptoed to the bedroom door and quietly turned the doorknob, peering into the corridor shyly. When she was certain there was no one around she sneaked down the corridor towards the staircase that led down to the back door, the one used for deliveries for the kitchen. She paused when she reached the staircase and strained her ears for any noises that might give her a clue to whether the path she was about to take was clear, or if she was going to get caught. She waited a few seconds more and tiptoed down the narrow stone steps and into the kitchen. *What if she is waiting for me down there? What if I can never leave? What if she hurts John?*

Bella pushed on, down the stairs, through the empty kitchen and reached the back door. She sighed with relief when she approached the thick wooden door to her freedom. Ecstatic that she had made it this far without being detected, the girl pulled the door with all her might. It was locked. She began to panic, nausea rising in her like the inevitable dawn. She slunk back into the kitchen and into the head chef's office where she was hoping to find a key to the door, she knew he had one somewhere, she was just hoping it wasn't with him.

Then it dawned on her, where were all the kitchen staff? Why was it so empty down here? Suddenly she felt trapped like a rat in one of the chef's traps. She walked back towards the staircase, hoping that she could back track and find another way out, a window on one of the upper floors maybe, when she heard sounds approaching, people approaching.

"We have to find that bloody girl, Catherine is going to have someone killed if she doesn't turn up soon and I bloody well don't want it to be me." Said one man.

"She could be long gone by now, what's the point lookin' for her eh? If she's still in the 'ouse she'll get hungry at some point and must come out, won't she?" Said a second man. The footsteps were edging closer to her, she tiptoed urgently back into the kitchen and panicked, looking around manically for a hiding place. She studied the length of the main room and saw a linen basket full of dirty laundry that would be sent away to be cleaned, as the staff didn't have the facilities to clean the amount generated by Lady Catherine and her guests, she hopped inside the basket and covered herself with just enough material that she *could breathe but also enough that she wouldn't be detected. Since the basket was out then, it meant the laundry was going to be sent away early the next morning, Bella had been paying attention to all the inner workings of the house when she wasn't being groomed by Catherine, she had memorised everything to do with the house and the staff in the months she had been kept prisoner there since she'd nothing better to fill her time with.*

Bella heard muffled voices and noises coming from near her hiding place, it sounded like the chef was making supper, she began to relax after a while as she was sure no one would find her in the basket. After the noises of the kitchen died away and she was almost certain the staff had gone to bed, the girl began to think about her escape, once more filled with hope. She fell asleep dreaming of being wheeled out the door right under everyone's noses, to her freedom.

Belladonna awoke once more, the blood in her head pounding in her ears and body aching. The room she was in was clinically bright, she lifted her arm to shield her eyes from the blinding light and waited for her eyes to focus. Once her eyesight returned to her she inspected the room, turning her aching head from side to side, it was like nowhere she had ever seen before. Clean white surfaces that appeared to be perfectly flat surrounded the edges of the room, on them were shiny devices and implements she couldn't even dream up a use for.

Confused she sat up, instantly regretting it as sharp stabbing pains ricocheted around her body, she gasped in pain.

"Woah there, stay still." A voice said from behind her, the girl looked around to see the owner of the voice and saw a middle-aged woman with silver hair and shining eyes smiling back at her. The woman was wearing white clothes, like the colour of chalk and nothing like the girl had ever seen on earth before. "You have been through hell, you need to rest little lady." The woman's voice was familiar and comforting, Bella laid back down on the bed and tried to think. Her head was spinning with questions. *What was she to ask first? How was she to approach this situation? Where the hell was she?*

"We understand you have no recollection of who you really are, is that correct?" The woman said, her voice cracked with emotion. Bella shook her head. *Who's we?* She thought.

"You also do not know what this place is?" She continued. Another head shake.

"Well…" Said the woman, after an uncomfortably long pause she walked round to the foot of the bed where Bella was lying. "Do you want to?"

Bella sat up in bed quickly, suddenly aware of how vulnerable she was to this woman, she was dressed in what appeared to be a thin white dress and she had no weapons and nothing to write with. Bella gestured with her hands asking the woman for a pencil and paper to write on. The woman looked confused.

"Why do you want paper?" She asked, still confused. Bella smiled, *she thought she had done her research but clearly, she didn't dig deep enough,* the woman passed over a pencil and paper, she began writing immediately. She handed the paper back to the woman.

After the woman had read the note she slowly looked up from the page with tears streaming down her pale cheeks, she began to sob heavily and collapsed to the ground, the note clutched to her chest, close to her heart. It was at this precise moment when three heavily armed guards garbed head to toe in black burst in through the seemingly invisible door.

"Seize her, no one is supposed to be in here!" Barked the first guard. The other two men in black grabbed the weeping woman off the floor and began escorting her out, ignoring her sobs. Bella could just make out the words she was saying between racking sobs as she allowed herself to be carted from the room.

"My baby…. My baby…. My baby…………"

***

After the guards had disappeared back through the invisible door with the sobbing woman in their arms, a man appeared, he was a lot younger than the woman probably in his mid-twenties and had short straight ashy blond hair, he smiled dryly at Bella when he entered.

"Hello, sorry for that intrusion. I take it you are comfortable enough?" He said as he approached the bed. Bella looked down at the strange heavy cast on her leg and nodded, surprisingly she was in a hell of a lot less pain than she was in before she woke up in the strange white room. "I oversee all new admissions to the Castle; my name is Abel. We understand that you are a mute, yes?" She nodded her head again. *This guy is an idiot. Just keep cool Bella, play the game.* She thought to herself. The man gestured to the pencil and paper. "I am sure you have some questions, fire away." He said with that repulsive smile slapped on his face.

What do you want with me? Where am I? What happened at the trial by combat? If you don't answer my questions, I won't cooperate with whatever you want me to do, there was a reason I was brought here right?

"Ah." Abel's demeanour changed immediately after

reading the note, from friendly and ignorant to smug and almost intimidating. She was right to play along and not stab him in the neck with her pencil. He crudely dragged a chair up to near the bed and slouched onto it. "They said you were smart, but people always underestimate you, don't they?"

Bella sat there for a moment contemplating her next move, she looked up at the man and innocently nodded. She didn't mean for this to provoke him, but it did.

"I have a fun game; it's called cooperate with us and we won't kill your friends. How does that sound?" Abel smiled smugly. Bella nodded once more. *Gods,* she thought, *what's going on in this place?*

Abel slid off his chair and grabbed one of the shiny devices from the immaculately white sides and twirled it in his hands menacingly.

"We want to know what's in your head, you see, you lived here with us a very long time ago and now you are back, stronger and more determined than anyone we have ever exiled from the castle. We want to know why, we want to know why you aren't a broken husk of a person like all the others and despite your strong reaction to the formula, how you have thrived and survived out there on your own all these years. You are our most spectacular lab rat! Isn't it fantastic how everything has come full circle? Well maybe not for your poor mother and father, or you for that matter, but the most important thing is that we won't make the same mistake twice." Abel said maniacally, with the passion and deliberateness of a madman.

Same mistake twice?

"Ah yes sorry, what I mean is that you won't get to

leave here alive. After already being influenced by the formula you won't react to it again in the same way and we can't have you leaving here knowing everything you know, can we?" He replied jovially.

What formula are you on about? Why would me leaving be such a problem for you people, I still have no idea what I am doing here or what this place even is! If you would be so kind as to stop being so cryptic and give me some actual answers for once that would be much appreciated.

Chapter Eleven
The Cells

The cells were every bit as strange as the room Bella had woken up in, she had spent a lot of time in cells in the past and these weren't them. White walls, white metal bars, bright white lamps that didn't look like they were burning at all, which was one of the stranger things that she had seen all day. As soon as Abel had finished taunting her, he had his guards carry her to her cell. Carried, because of her broken leg, a lovely parting gift from the dead bully of her previous residence.

"You will be here until we can figure out what to do with you." Said the guard as he manhandled her into the immaculate cell. She rolled her eyes and watched as he slid the bars across the door frame. There hadn't been a cell that she hadn't been able to escape from, confidently she slumped against the back wall and began studying the room for weaknesses.

"Abel will be here when they have reached a decision." Said a voice from the next cell over. Bella had to do a double take because all she saw was a white brick wall, with a small slit big enough to slide a letter through, just near the corner joint of the cell. Abel had confiscated her paper and pen before throwing her in these stupidly bright cells, so she would have to just ignore her new neighbour. These bright lamps were annoying Bella, there were no shadows, Bella loved the shadows, all assassins loved the shadows, there were places to hide but, in that cell, there was nowhere that she could hide, and it made her feel more vulnerable than she had felt in a very long time. The guards could see everything from their inquisitive desk opposite the cells.

Bella wrestled herself to her feet quickly despite the agonisingly rigid position of her leg, the cast was thigh high and was very difficult to manoeuvre especially since they didn't give her any crutches. *Perfect,* she thought, *they are making sure I am weak.* After what felt like an hour of being sat down she hopped over to the metal barred door of her cell, nonchalantly. After studying the door quickly, she realised that there was no keyhole, why was there no keyhole? How does the door lock without a key, is the door even locked? Then it hit her, she hadn't even seen the guard lock the door with a key, how could she have possibly missed something like that! Normally she was unnaturally perceptive, she blamed the lamps for dulling her senses. She reached out curiously and grabbed one of the metal bars on the door ready to slide it freely open but as soon as her skin made contact with the metal her body was flooded with white hot crackling pain like she had never felt before, she was knocked back gasping in disbelief.

What the hell? She thought as she cradled her frazzled arm to her body like a protective mother would her baby. A guard laughed.

"Not from around here are you?" Said the mysterious voice from the next cell over.

"That is enough Adele, shut it." Said the guard at the desk, shooting a warning look at the mysterious speaker. "She's a bloody mute, no point talking to her."

"She can listen though can't she." Adele scoffed, in pure defiance of the authority.

"Last warning shut it!" Spat the guard, thankfully

she had enough common sense to do what the guard said this time.

Bella slumped back against the wall and sighed in defeat, clutching her stinging hand. It did not look like she was going to get out of these cells under her own steam as she had previously thought, all there was to do was wait. So, she waited.

She must have fallen asleep because the next thing she knew the mechanical sound of the cell door sliding open was penetrating her ears. She snapped her eyes open and scrambled to her feet again, still weak from her injuries at the trial and the stinging of her frazzled hand threw off her balance and she pitched forward clumsily. The guard saw this as an aggressive attack and slammed his baton down hard on Bella's back, it crunched on impact and sent her quickly to the cell floor, well quicker than she was already heading. She attempted to blink the woozy pain from her head and looked up fuzzily at the intruders to her cell.

"What the hell Des, she's injured you know." Said one of the other guards, crossing the cell to help Bella up.

"She tried to attack me!" Said the one called Des.

"She was just trying to stand up, stop being so trigger happy. Gosh newbies, am I right?" Said the other guard. The joke didn't land with the rest of the invasion party and she was dragged out of her cell in silence. Less woozy than before the guards had picked her up, she tried to investigate the cell next to hers to see the mysterious Adele. The cell was occupied by what Bella thought was a young woman in her late teens or perhaps early twenties, with dirty blonde hair and extraordinarily plain features.

The mystery woman stared back at her from behind

the white metal bars and shock was plastered over those plain features as she saw Bella, she rose to her feet and crossed the cell in a heartbeat.

"Margot." She cried, "Margot! It's me Adelaide!" She was brimming with pained happiness as she screamed the words, until she saw the confusion on Bella's face; Adele crumpled into a heap on the floor of her cell, visibly heartbroken and unable to utter another word as Bella was dragged unresisting away.

The guards carried Bella out of the cell block and into the bright morning sun. It was somehow even brighter than the lamps in the cell block, which until this moment she thought was impossible. The brightness was probably being intensified by bouncing off all the white or glass buildings, she had officially changed her mind about the lights being the strangest thing she had seen in this place, annoyed that that fact kept changing she focussed instead on soaking up her surroundings.

"Ah there she is!" Abel bellowed, arms thrown out wide as if presenting the girl at a cattle auction. This was when Bella noticed that there was a gaggle of people standing behind him, which is when she really did feel like she was a prize cow at auction. People gasped and murmured as she was dragged up to Abel, where she was immediately un-handed by the guards. Bella shot them a warning look that said *just wait til I am better, and you won't live to see another day if you treat me like that again.*

"Want us to cuff her, Abel?" Said Des, clearly the most paranoid guard. Or the smartest. Always be wary of strangers, duh.

"No Desmond, that will not be necessary, will it?" Abel replied, the last part being directed at Bella who shook her head dutifully. *Play their game,* she thought to herself, *and you'll be out of here in no time.*

The guard's half carried, half led her into a building that was ridiculously tall and made almost completely of glass, a building that wouldn't last two minutes in the real world. They took her into a small room where a long smooth table dominated the centre, surrounded by lots of comfortable looking chairs. Everyone sat down in what seemed like a premeditated seating arrangement, leaving one chair free for their guest. She was seated between an elderly man with silver hair and red glasses and a middle-aged woman with auburn hair, Bella noticed that she was wearing trousers. She liked this because people should be able to wear what they want and not have social constructs barring them from doing so, anyway trousers were more practical and Bella was pleased to see that the women in this strange society were being treated much better than they were where Bella grew up. This was when she noticed that everyone in the room was wearing bizarre outfits, the sorts that she had never seen before. She shook her head lightly at the impracticality of some of the clothes she saw, none of these people would stand a chance in these clothes if they had to spend a few days on the road, as they were all wildly impractical. But that seemed to be a running theme with this place.

"Okay quiet down everyone, as you all know we have voted to keep… Belladonna and let her join our community here at the Castle." Abel said, pausing to study the various nods and agreements around the room. "She will be assigned work as soon as her wounds heal, in the meantime she will need to rest up and get used to our way of life before taking her career aptitude test and her transition into our community begins. Any questions?"

"Where will she live? Some people might not feel so safe with an outsider living so freely amongst us, you know that Abel. We don't know anything about her, who knows who she was out there, she could be a killer for all we know." Said the elderly, no, ancient woman, who sat at the head of the table. Bella had to resist the urge to smile, what they don't know won't hurt them, right? This caused a murmur to spread around the table infectiously.

"Calm down everyone, okay, calm down. She's not a murderer, she's a young girl. Give her the benefit of the doubt, we voted to let her stay here and join our community. So, show some respect, she is one of us and you know it. She was born here just like the rest of you. She will be living in Mrs Cockers house, god rest her soul. With, erm, Adele? They need to learn to be upstanding members of this society and hopefully they can learn together. All in agreement raise your hands." Abel paused again to count all those in favour, "An eight-three split in agreement, any more questions?" Abel continued to ramble on. Bella was taken aback by what he had said about her being born here, she wanted to know what the hell was going on and why everyone seemed to be more in the loop about her life than she was!

While they were talking, Bella stared out of the window at the courtyard below and got lost in a world of her own.

The girl ran, giggling, away from another girl. This other girl was much taller, and would no doubt catch up to the smaller girl because she had much longer legs and besides that she was more competitive than the younger girl, whose pitch-black hair was streaming proudly behind her like a flag.

The older girl's hair wasn't as beautiful as the black-haired girl's and she loathed her for it, people always loved and doted on her younger sister more than they ever had on her. Comparing her to Snow White, the beautiful fictional princess from the old stories. The older girl's hair was a dull light brown, dark blonde colour that she hated because it was not the rich deep brown of their fathers but a sapped, lifeless version instead. And that is exactly how she felt compared to her little sister.

Finally, the older girl caught up to her sister and slapped her on the back hard and exclaimed.

"Tag, you're it!" Laughing, she loved beating her sister at these games. It was the only time she felt true happiness.

"Hey!" The younger sister shrieked as she crumpled to the ground under her sisters' heavy hand. She didn't cry when she hit the ground or even when she saw the gravel stuck bloodily in her porcelain palms.

"Margot! Are you alright, I am so sorry I didn't mean to be that rough." Cried the older sister as she pulled the Margot to her feet.

"I know, it's fine it wasn't your fault the ground was bumpy." Said the young girl defensively.

"Adelaide! Margot!" Screamed a shrill voice from nearby.

"Busted." Whispered Adelaide to her younger sister as she squeezed her tightly for a second before the owner of the shrill voice reached them. It was the girls' nanny Ms Appleby, the meanest old bag on the planet, or so the girls' thought at the time.

"What on earth do you two think you are doing!" Ms Appleby shrieked, "Oh Margot, what's happened to your hands?" Grasping the girl's hands firmly in her own and examining them thoroughly, Margot winced as she did this and Ms Appleby turned on Adelaide accusingly.

"We were just playing Ms Appleby, she fell." Adelaide mumbled to the woman's feet.

"You need to be more careful Adelaide, more responsible for your sister, she is only six years old for goodness sakes. Now straight upstairs before the guards find us trespassing and throw us all in the cells." She said ushering the girls away from their beloved play haven, which they adored so much because it was the only place in the whole compound that made them feel like they were outside in the real world, the world outside the confines of the Castle.

After the meeting Bella was finally gifted some light metal crutches and escorted through the village with Abel acting like a tour guide pointing out key buildings and generally rambling on about the history of the place, none of which she found very interesting, or interesting enough to pay attention to. What she did want to know however was more personal,

Who am I?

Who was the girl from her memory?

What did Abel mean when he said I was born here?

Nothing about her life had ever made sense but she had made her peace with that, until coming here and being bombarded with new information and confusion.

"Here we are." Abel said, penetrating her thought bubble. She snapped back into focus and saw a quaint cottage sandwiched between two tall glass buildings. "Mrs Cocker never wanted the building to modernise, she was very old fashioned. We thought it might be more to your taste than the other buildings we have here." This wasn't the Abel she had met when she had woken up, the narcissistic know it all that saw right through her, just like she saw right through him. He was putting on an act for these people, he lied to them

114

about who she really was. Or does that mean he was lying to her about her birthplace instead? Bella's head was pounding with questions. She knew two things though; one, he confiscated her writing supplies to keep her in the dark and two, he knew she could expose him for who he really was.

The inside of the house was plainly furnished much like the cottage she grew up in with Hazel, Maple and Juniper all those years ago. Except this place was cleaner and less cluttered - the opposite of the homely and well lived in one she knew.

"I suppose you want to know what's really going on here, huh? Why did I get you out of the cells and, making you play house?" Abel, the real Abel, said bluntly. Ah there he was, thought Bella. She nodded cautiously. "Sit down." She did as she was told and sat down on a comfortable looking but very firm beige settee. "Spoiler alert! You were born here, in the Castle. You even have parents and a sister here, so I wouldn't try and pull any of your stunts in case you became the orphan you already thought you were. When you were a young girl, about seven or eight I think. You were banished from our community because of your traitorous parents, as a punishment for them you see. But you were never supposed to live, it's a miracle." Abel said perched calmly on the corner of the dining room table, clearly enjoying himself. "We wiped your memory and dumped you in the woods. That's why you don't remember anything about the Castle, including your family. But we must have used too much serum because we never expected, well, these results." He cackled menacingly. Bella could feel the heat rising in her like a volcano about to erupt, he was goading her, and it was working. She wanted to kill him, and it would be so easy for her to do, though not so easy to get away from in this place. And if what he was saying about her family was true, then she would really have to be on her best behaviour for their sakes. He wanted her to attack him, it would be the perfect excuse to silence her, for good this time. She balled up her hands into tight fists and clenched her jaw to remain calm, although calm wasn't her strong suit. She remembered back to the knife protruding from Bobby's hand. Bobby. She still felt his lifeless body weighing down on her like none of the other lives she had ever taken, she suddenly began to feel more trapped.

Bella took some deep breaths and forced herself to look up at Abel who was smiling down on her, his crazy eyes boring into her own.

"Smart girl, you worked it out, didn't you?" He said slowly leaning towards her, taunting her. She nodded stiffly. She really was trapped. "If you inform anyone of our little conversation and try to expose me then I will kill your family, okay? Oh no, I wouldn't harm a single hair on your head, you are my precious little miracle. Anyway, I'd want you to take some responsibility for your actions for once in your life." He stood up straight, brushed his greasy hair out of his face and composed himself before donning his fake smile and letting himself out of Bella's new home.

She exhaled shakily from anger. She had been so careful over the years making sure she never got close to anyone again, so they couldn't be ripped from her again, to make sure that she had no weakness'. And now look what happened, she suddenly had three weaknesses' just as she had come up against someone that needed taking down. She thought about Will and how she could have risked it all with him, how they could have been happy together if she hadn't been so reserved and afraid of losing people. She lost Will and now she had lost her freewill and morals, she couldn't let Abel get away with this. How many more people had he turned out into the real world with no memories of their old lives or families, how many lives had he ruined on his way to the top? She wondered whether Will ever thought of her, if he was even still alive. Her heart ached for the third time that day. She thought for a brief second that Abel could be bluffing to control her, but she dismissed it immediately. There was too much at stake for her to think that.

She sat on her own in silence until she realised the gnawing pain in her stomach wasn't just anxiety and nausea at the thought of being trapped so easy, it was also hunger. She got up from the settee and hobbled into the kitchen where she started pulling open cupboards randomly and browsing their contents, pots, pans, plates, cups, glasses. They were all matching sets in impeccable condition which Bella had never seen before and found it strangely uncomfortable. She was also confused about the white humming cupboard under the counter top, so she thought she better leave that one alone, who knows what could be in there. Bees?

She found some bread in a wooden box on the counter top, already sliced! After some more rummaging she found a jar of jam. She took her haul back to her settee and began making jam sandwiches whilst trying to ignore all the strange things she could see. A stove with no compartment for fuel, no wood pile, no burning lamps, no larder but a giant black picture frame with no picture in it. *A very bizarre centrepiece*, she thought.

Bella was in the middle of these rambling thoughts when she heard the front door open. She grabbed the nearest thing she could reach that wasn't her jam sandwich as a weapon, a metal vase with a lid. *Strange,* she thought, *where the hell do the flowers go.* She stood up with her weapon and hid behind the wall separating the kitchen and the living room, weapon at the ready, trying to make as little noise as she could while juggling the light crutches and her much heavier, substantial weapon.

"Hello!" A voice called from the doorway. Bella was confused, intruders didn't usually announce themselves on entrance to the property. She rounded the corner, lowering her weapon slightly. Stood in the doorway, was the crazy girl from the cells, Adele.

"Those are Mrs Cockers ashes!" Exclaimed Adele, who put her hands up to her face in shock and defence. Bella looked from the metal vase in her hand and thought, *an urn, that makes way more sense.* She put it down on the kitchen counter and shot an apologetic look over at the girl that said, sorry for trying to kill you with someone else's bodily remains. Anyway, who keeps that as a decoration in the house they used to live in? She shivered none the less and wiped her hands on her tunic, that she was glad to have finally got back from Abel after being trapped in that weird white dress. It was at that moment when Bella realised that this was the girl from the memory she had earlier in the conference room, this place was getting to be a horrible trigger for memories. That was when it hit her, this was only the second memory she had from before she lost her memories, *does that mean the serum is wearing off? Will I ever get all my memories back?* She thought.

"So, you can't speak, huh?" Adele said from the safety of the doorway. This snapped Bella out of her trance and she shook her head. "And you don't remember me?" Bella shook her head again, ashamed of the pain it was causing the other girl. Adele exhaled deeply, she was wringing her hands uncontrollably, Bella noticed. She definitely wasn't being put up to this, Bella could always tell what people's body language was saying how they really felt about a situation, the spaces between the words tell you a lot more about a person than words themselves sometimes. Although Bella wished she had her writing supplies because then comforting the girl would be much easier.

Bella took Adele's hand, dragged her into the living room and sat her down so they were facing each other on the same beige settee. Bella put her hand meaningfully on Adele's shoulder and smiled reassuringly. Comforting someone wasn't really Bella's strong suit, she never stuck around long enough to be good at it.

"Okay so where do I begin, my name is Adelaide King, daughter of Diane and Maxwell King. Our name carries, well... used to carry weight around here until, well... the coup and until my little sister, Margot King was...Taken. From. Us." She said the last words slowly, letting each one sink in before uttering the next. She looked up at Bella, she had finally stopped wringing her hands.

Bella drew in a sharp breath of stale air. *Of course,* she thought, *only her and that crazy woman had recognised me since I got here and oh my god, that crazy woman...* She let her thoughts trail off. She looked up into her sisters' pale blue eyes and saw years of pain buried behind them, that fresh pain however began to leak out and spill down her face freely. Bella shook her head apologetically which only made her sister sob harder, she scooted closer and wrapped her arms around Adele, who buried her face into her younger sisters' shoulder. *I am so sorry,* Bella thought, wishing her sister could hear her, *I am so sorry.*

King, she thought, *what an interesting name, a coincidence since the place we live is called the Castle.* And that's when it hit her, Adele did say that the name used to carry weight around the place. Surely her life wouldn't be one of those long-lost princess clichés from a de-throned royal family. Abel the usurper had to die now.

Bella untangled herself from her sister's warm embrace and stood up in search of writing supplies or anything she could use as writing supplies. She returned to her confused looking sister ten minutes later with a book and a pencil carefully stashed in the old woman's sewing box.

"Margot what on earth are you doing?" Adele said, leaning in to look at why her sister was defiling a book. No blank paper was to be found, not even a blank page in the damn book so Bella began circling words appropriate to build her message to her sister, Bella relaxed as she sat circling words frantically, being able to finally communicate was making her feel more hopeful and connected to her long-lost family member. She passed the finished article over to Adele who sat trying to piece together the puzzle, what words couldn't be easily found in the book were crammed into the spaces between lines in Bella's beautiful handwriting.

My name is Belladonna, I was given this name by my guardians, three old women I lived with in the first part of my new life. Until they were killed by witch hunters. I woke up without my memory and my voice, I couldn't even remember what night was which made for a very interesting few days of my new life. No wonder babies cry so much when they are born, waking up in a strange and dark world is traumatizing. The Castle erased my memories hoping that I would die in the woods that day, but I never gave up on life, I always felt that I had some unfinished business I had to complete first. Which led me here. I don't think they can reverse what they did to me, but I know that we can take the Castle down, I have a plan, but we need to be careful and we need to work together. You in?

I also have some questions to ask you. I think I saw our mother earlier today, what did our parents do that was so bad I was banished? Why is Abel in charge? And you are going to have to tell me all the security features of this place in detail, and if you have time some stories of our childhood would be great too.

I know this is a lot for you to take in, it is a lot for me too. I just want you to know that I am truly sorry for the years we never got to spend together and for the years I don't recall. I hope I can make it all up to you when this is all done. You must keep calling me Margot because Abel can't know that you know my real name because I'm not supposed to be communicating with you.

All my love, Margot.

It took Adele a while to sift through the book and digest the meaning of the note, in that time Bella helped herself to more homemade jam sandwiches and studied her sister's face while she read the words she had been so desperate to part with all day. She smiled a sad smile and let loose the last few stragglers from her tear ducts.

"Oh Margot, you always did try and take care of me even when you were little. It's my turn now, to look after you like I should have been doing this whole time, I'm in. What's the plan?" Adele said to her little sister, the look of defiance in her eyes was the same one that Bella had been told she had all her life.

Chapter Twelve
Prison, Sweet Prison

It had been three weeks since the sisters had hatched out their plan for escape and it was in full swing. Bella hopped her way through the immaculate streets of the Castle's compound on her crutches and smiled sweetly at the other residents. She hated every second of it, she had thought the Guild was making her weak, but this place was so much worse. She felt like she was both being wrapped in cotton wool and kept on her toes at the same time, it was a very uncomfortable combination. The girls had decided to wait until Bella had fully recovered from her trial by combat before initiating the final phase of the plan, the one that required running. And a lot of it.

"Ah Margot I see you are doing the usual rounds this morning?" Said one of the sweet old men that spent all his time in his little patch of garden, he was called Hank. Bella had been assigned as a messenger for the corporate staff of the Castle, this meant she had written notes and delivered them wherever they needed to go. She was slow but at least she didn't gossip which was apparently why the last messenger was... fired. Bella just smiled and nodded sweetly to Hank and hopped away. She hated the way people were always watching her, she had always thought that Hank was spying on her and reporting back to Abel. One thing she knew however was that this place was making her paranoid.

It was midday before she had finished her rounds, something that would have taken her an hour to do if she was in her usual state of fitness. Adele was waiting in the living room of their shared prison for her to return, poised on the edge of the settee like she had done every day since her arrival. Waiting for the short period of time they had alone together, the time they used to check in with each other and shared intel. Abel had made sure that the sisters only saw each other for less than an hour a day, keeping them busy with odd jobs that meant they were hardly ever in the same place at one given time, this was very clever Bella had to admit.

"Hey, new record! You are getting speedy on those crutches sis." Adele broke into a huge smile, even though they never shared many conversations the sisters had become really close during the short time they had been reunited. Bella just shook her head and smirked. She had to admit even though they were technically prisoners, she was the happiest she had ever been. "Okay so this morning I learned that the council's nervous about something out there." Adele continued. *Out there,* that's what people in the Castle compound called the real world and it annoyed Bella every time she heard it. Bella nodded attentively. "I don't know what is going on out there, but it seems to have them really spooked, do you have any idea what might have happened to make them so on edge?" Adele looked worried and excited at the same time, this could just be the moment they had been waiting for, a distraction from the outside would be the perfect moment to carry out the final part of their plan.

Bella shook her head slowly, closing her eyes and straining her memory. *Who could make them that scared?* Then it hit her, the Assassins Guild. She knew that there was always pressure on the Guild from an outside source, but she didn't know it was the Castle, maybe they were angry that the Guild was raided. *Maybe they are coming to rescue me.* Bella snapped her eyes open and stared at her sister who was waiting in anticipation, Bella nodded slowly. She had refrained from telling her sister about her life, which wasn't hard without the ability to write, so technically she wasn't actually lying to her. Bella had never felt this nauseated by a potential conversation before, but at that moment in time she was unbelievably nervous about telling her big sister that she killed people for a living.

***

"Yooohoooo!" Cried Abel through the open cottage door, Adele sighed into her hands, he was not the person that she was waiting so anxiously for.

"What is it Abel?" She said, as the obnoxious figure sauntered into the living room, a cocky smile playing on his thin lips.

"Oh, now, now Adelaide dearest, that is no way to speak to someone who just wants to help you. Is it?" He said lowering himself onto the sofa next to Adele.

"Go on then I'll bite, how are you going to *help* me today Abel?" She said giving him a sarcastically sweet smile in return. He slid closer to her on the sofa and chuckled.

"I have some information about dearest little sister that you might just find…. *Fascinating.*" His face erupted into a devilish grin that made Adele inadvertently shrink away from him.

***

Week five of imprisonment in the Castle was when

Bella started to lose her patience, it had been over two weeks since the weird tension began to spread through the Castle and nothing had come of it. It was driving Bella crazy, coupled with the fact that Adele had not taken the news of her sisters' previous life too well, she was not enjoying life in the Castle anymore. She hobbled her usual route through the town, delivering letters and smiling at the elderly spies sent to watch her every move. She played the dejected looking prisoner who knew she would spend the rest of her days trapped in everyone else's paradise, when really, she was plotting her escape in every waking moment. There had been more letters and more meetings in the last week and she was really hoping she would overhear something useful or something would kick off, but it never did. Instead she crutched her way through the maze of glass buildings, she knew every inch of the compound and there was only one entrance that she knew of and it was the most fortified and heavily guarded gate she had ever seen in her life. There was no way she would be able to sneak out of the compound, the only way they would be able to leave was basically a suicide mission disguised as hope.

"Ah just the person I was hoping to run into." Said a shy but strangely familiar voice by Bella's side. She spun around to see who was ambling next to her. He lowered his voice to barely a whisper and continued. "Don't be alarmed, don't act surprised, just smile. They're always watching." Said the man who had once broken into her room at the Guild. The man who had not only changed her life but how she looked at the world, forever.

Declan Winters.

"I was undercover in the Guild and they brought

me back today because they are rallying the troops, if you know what I mean. The Castle are preparing for an attack. What I told you before about how you were to play a role in this is going to come to pass sooner than you think, and you need to seize that opportunity. I'm glad you made it out alive by the way, I heard it was one hell of a fight." He smiled nervously and continued to keep Bella's agonisingly slow pace. She was so sick of the inconveniently long cast that she was debating just ripping it off herself. She was in awe at what Declan had just said but tried not to show it on her face, she just smiled and nodded like you would if a random crazy person just started talking to you and you wanted to get rid of them - while not appearing to be rude or uninterested.

She had a newfound respect for the awkward man ambling beside her, she had just assumed he was spineless and paranoid for no reason, now she saw he was actually a double agent for the Guild and had been risking his life this whole time.

"Oh, and another thing, all the Winters have been called back to the Castle. Including the man that sold you as a slave to a crazy woman when you were eight years old, thought I'd give you a heads up. Don't let it ruin your opportunity to end all this though, pick your battles carefully Margot." And then he peeled off into the largest of the glass buildings. *The Castle is going to be attacked? Winters is back? He called me Margot! So he did know who I was all along and didn't tell me, I swear if I ever see him again I'll rip out his tongue.*

Bella was fuming and still reeling from her strange encounter, with the man who explained to her what happened in the apocalypse a couple of months ago, when suddenly she crashed into a woman. The two of them went sprawling to the ground in a heap of limbs. The woman swore as she collided with the ground and knocked the air out of Bella.

"Watch where you're walking!" Screeched the disgruntled woman tangled in crutches and limbs, she looked at Bella and gasped. "Oh gods, I am so sorry. I didn't realise it was you." She said as she untangled herself and helped Bella to her feet. She carefully reunited Bella with her mail bag and crutches, Bella just smiled and hobbled away. *What the hell was that about? First, she shouts at me and then she's all apologetic? And what did she mean by I didn't realise it was* you. *This place is getting weirder and weirder by the day.*

After Bella's strange morning she returned to her small cottage on the outskirts of the compound. Her sister was waiting for her like a loyal hound, as she did every day, despite learning of her harrowed past.

"You're late." Adele said, wringing her hands. Bella gave her an apologetic smile and proceeded to fill her in on the events of the morning through scribbling between the lines of the book they had found. They were running out of space quickly. Adele sat in silence for a while, processing the new information. Ever since Abel had told Adele about Bella's life before being reunited with her sister she had been a little off with her and her temper had grown increasingly shorter.

"So, we were right, they are expecting an attack. Do you think it is from the Guild as they have brought back that Declan guy? Or are they just protecting their own people. GAH! I am so sick of this." She spiralled quickly, her frustration got the better of her and she stormed upstairs. It had been happening a lot more recently, Adele's hot temper was becoming an issue.

Bella got up and made the two of them their usual

dinner, sandwiches and a cup of tea; and waited for her sister to return. It took her longer to calm down today as every growing mystery was taking its toll on her patience. She smiled at the sandwiches on the coffee table and joined her sister.

"I'm sorry, I know all of this is literally not your fault but it's just getting to me. I want to leave this place and live our own lives without people watching us constantly and controlling our every move." Adele said through bites of her sandwich. Bella nodded into her own sandwich and placed her free hand on the older girl's shoulder comfortingly. *Me too sis, me too.* Bella had never wanted to talk to someone so much in her life, there was so much to say, so much they didn't know about each other. Bella hadn't even got the chance to meet their parents properly since being kidnapped and she was growing ever concerned that something bad had happened to them, she couldn't be sure that they were still alive, and she wasn't willing to jeopardize Adele's freedom for it.

"Good news, though right? We might not have to wait much longer for our distraction, eh?" Adele smiled, she always liked to put a sarcastically optimistic spin on things. They both knew that it was unlikely they would both get out of the compound alive, but they also knew it would be better than staying trapped there forever. They would both risk their lives in the post-apocalyptic mess that was the real world than stay in *paradise* two minutes longer. After Bella had told Adele about Declan and how he had quickly taught her about the demise of the planet, Adele had filled her in on the rest of the details.

"So yeah, Declan and the book you read were right, the world as everyone knew it ended. Those humans that survived only survived because they were lucky, they had storm shelters or bunkers of some sort that meant they missed the super volcano exploding and the whole volcanic winter thing, they were extremists or rich people that had planned and been stockpiling for this event for years. *Doomsday preppers.* They waited out the worst of it and then surfaced when they had run out of food and other supplies, they became lawless and the world was chaotic for many, many years until... The Castle.

They knew that the world couldn't continue as it had been pre-apocalypse because humans had already drained the world of its resources, they also knew that the world couldn't continue as it had been post-apocalypse either because people were wiping each other out just as quickly as the famine had years before. So, they created an enforced law, and have been in charge ever since. They deprive the people of technology and development because they are scared of what they will do with it. They have become cowards hiding in their ivory tower. The law pretty much runs itself now and no one out there has any recollection of what happened generations ago, people don't seem to care, they like the order that The Castle provides.

Generations have lived under their rule, generations have been oppressed by their elitism and it must stop. The world ended for god's sake and people are still being as selfish as they were when they caused the apocalypse!

Oh and it is incredibly rare that you got to read an actual book about it though, because all the books were burned so that none of them got into the hands of the people and a revolution was started, the fact that the guild has a whole library is enough to get them all killed. The whole reason the Castle exists is so that people on the outside never get back to the same level of technological advancement that caused the world to purge itself again. It is kind of sad when you think about it...

Anyway, that is pretty much what happened out there, except I've been hearing talk that there is a resistance on the outside and that some of the residents here agree with it! That's good news, right?" Adele said beaming. Bella smiled back and composed her response on the limited paper they had left.

Woah that is a lot to take in, thank you for sharing that with me. I have my concerns about this alleged resistance within the Castle, I think they are just trying to draw out traitors before whatever attack they have planned. So please, please, please be careful and don't talk to anyone else about our escape plan or join the resistance because we have a much better chance on our own. I can protect you, but not if you go gallivanting off with some so-called resistance.

Before Adele could utter a response there was a knock at the door. The sisters looked at each other like they had seen a ghost. For weeks now they had been worried that someone was listening to their conversations in the cottage, Adele said that she had already checked the place for bugs but Bella didn't know what that meant, she kept an eye out for eavesdroppers round the cottage before any big plans were being made.

"Come in!" Shouted Adele from the settee, Bella gave her a warning glance before the visitor entered their cottage.

"Don't worry ladies, it is just me. Abel!" Said a chirpy, well dressed Abel. "I have come here today to invite you both to an execution, how exciting!" He smiled maniacally at the pair and clapped his hands in front of him in excitement.

"I'm sorry, what?" Adele blurted, mouth agape.

"Oh sorry, your invitations must have got lost in the mail…" He said, giving Bella a slimy wink.

"Who's execution?" Adele whispered. Abel smirked, his eyes glinting.

"Hurry up and get dressed, I've brought you some nice clothes to wear. You will join me and the other council members for the event, so you need to look presentable." He said reaching around the front door to procure two dress boxes.

After Abel's last impromptu visit, Adele had dreaded him seeing her and Bella in the same room together in case he tried to pry them apart. Even after the details about Bella's past had been revealed there was no way she was going to abandon her little sister after everything that they'd been through. How long had it had taken for them to find each other? It didn't matter how worried she was that her baby sister was a trained assassin.

It made her think about her own chequered past and the things that she had had to do to survive, even within the confines of the Castle walls. She wondered if Abel had pulled the same trick on Bella and told her about her past… About what happened at the nunnery, the thought of which made her subconsciously rub the leather arm brace that covered her left forearm. She had always meant to tell her sister of the ordeals she had been through, in fact she had dreamt of the day when they could share their stories with each other, without judgement. But it all seemed so wrong now, her little sister had been through so much and had to do such horrible things to survive, it just wasn't the reunion she had been hoping for. She had long given up on ever finding her sister and now that she had her, she didn't want to dwell on the past any longer.

Chapter Thirteen
The Execution

Belladonna and Adelaide washed and changed into their fancy new dresses, reminding Bella of how she would be dressed up like a doll when she lived with Lady Catherine. She despised herself for letting this happen again. Together they made their way to the courtyard, Bella hobbling on her crutches and Adele ambling along beside her younger sister. The transformation of the courtyard into gallows made Bella feel sorry for the poor sucker they were going to off, nonetheless, they walked over to what they assumed was the council's box. An elevated seating area above the gallows and the common audience.

"Ooooh ladies you look magnificent! Let the party begin." Said Abel, uncomfortably excited at the prospect of another unjust death in the world. He led them over to their seats and introduced them to some of the other council members in the box, once he had done this he smirked. "Okay ladies and gentlemen I have to take care of something really quickly and then I will be back to enjoy the festivities!" Bella had never seen someone so excited for a hanging before, even in all the time she had spent on the street amongst gangs and thieves. He was something else.

The sisters sat uncomfortably in their white gowns, amongst people she despised, waiting for the execution of a most likely innocent person. She hated how weak she felt, how vulnerable this broken leg and a family had made her. She wished she had never had the chance to set foot in this bright, clean paradise. She preferred the grey tinged, once barren and derelict land on the outside; at least out there everyone was equal, and they built everything they had from scratch, this was just privilege at its worst. Then she remembered, she was raised in this privilege. The fact that she was one of them, the people she had despised when growing up made her feel physically sick.

People were beginning to file in one by one, muttering and gaping at the gallows in the centre of the courtyard, standing row by row behind the metal barriers like they were at a concert. It didn't take long for the whole courtyard to fill up with curious people, clearly, they knew as much about this than Bella and Adele had this morning. What could have happened for Abel to stage a sudden execution? Bella then began to think about the resistance and how the tension was building outside the Castle, she was right to tell Adele not to get involved with the resistance. She had a hunch that this might be a big show to make people fear the council and gain back some power, by publicly executing the leader of the resistance within the Castle itself.

On the gallows a man with a black hood began setting up ropes, ropes plural. There was going to be more than one execution by the look of it. Bella nudged Adele, getting her to look at the gallows. She raised her eyebrows questioningly.

"More than one? Who are they?" Whispered Adele, making sure no one overheard her. The sky was grey and overcast, which reminded Bella of home. Not the usual bright sunny day reflecting off the tall glass buildings, this gave the courtyard a sombre, macabre look. *Very fitting with the tone of the event*, Bella thought. She hoped it rained, with everyone in the courtyard at once and all their attention turned one way; it might just be the perfect chance to escape! Bella looked at Adele during this eureka moment but there was no way she could convey her plan. They hadn't come up with a signal that meant *GO!* Which was a huge oversight.

It was at this moment that Abel stepped up onto the stage with a shorter, squatter man with grey hair and round glasses.

"Can I get your attention please!" Abel's voice ricocheted through the courtyard with help from the microphone at the centre of the stage, the small man next to him looked like a squat guard dog. "I am now going to pass you over to our Chief of Justice Gustavo Cloyte! Give it up for Gus everybody!" Abel's cheery voice and bright suit contrasted with the rest of the world in a garish way, as he passed the microphone over to the Chief of Justice.

"Good afternoon everyone, sorry for the lack of publicity running up to the event, the ruling was only finalised this morning…" Gus barked down the microphone, Bella's ears pricked when she heard the man's voice. *It couldn't be the same man that wanted me dead in the Guild could it?* She closed her eyes and listened to the rest of the man's opening speech. *Son of a gun! It was him.* Things were starting to make much more sense to her now, coming to the Castle had filled in most of the missing pieces to her grand puzzle. She sighed, there was no way she could fill Adele in before the execution. Instead she sat still and well-behaved in the council members box hoping that it would rain. These people didn't look like the sort who would stand in the rain for an execution.

"… Bring out the damned!" Concluded Gus' speech. At this moment everyone in the box and the audience craned their necks to see the three hooded figures marching onto the gallows with their hands and feet bound, trying desperately to figure out who they were. Bella couldn't care less at this point who they were, there was no one here apart from the girl sitting next to her that she knew or cared about. She just wanted this to be over.

"Thank you, Gus. Now you know the charges, but do you know the people responsible? Before we reveal who they are I would just like to share a few words, a story about the condemned. As you know I am the rightful King of the Castle, I usurped the traitors before me and was very merciful, I let them live and that was a big mistake I tell you all now.

Let me tell you a story from my childhood to start with, I was raised here in the Castle, but I was kept quiet and under the radar because, well, my parents were ashamed of me. A sickly baby that probably wouldn't survive, they didn't want people to know that he would be the heir to their Kingdom, now would they? So, they sent me away." Abel stopped as his voice cracked with rage and emotion, but that wasn't the noise that caught Belladonna's attention. A low rumbling in the background that normal people might mistake for thunder booming miles away. Bella knew that wasn't the case this time, she grabbed Adele's arm and guided her out of the box, everyone's attention was glued on Abel, including Adele's. So, leaving was easy. Bella hobbled as fast as she could as near to the main gate as she dared, the two of them bobbed down behind a supply cart.

"What the hell Margot? You don't understand what he was saying do you?" Adele's eyes were spilling over with tears as she stared into the unwavering eyes of her sister. They could just make out Abel's voice booming through the compound.

"My dear old Mother and Father then had two beautiful daughters many years later who were poster girls for the throne. This left me, the eldest and rightful heir, now perfectly healthy, cheated out of his birth right!" Abel's voice was so full of emotion now the crowd was completely silent, and no one had realised the departure of the sisters, thunder boomed closer and the heavens began to open, but no one would dare move because they were enchanted by Abel's speech. "I AM ABEL KING!" They could hear the whole courtyard gasp and break out in murmurs. "So, Diane and Maxwell King, I charge you with treason again, for building a resistance within these walls and Declan Winters for being an accomplice to treason. You will all hang."

Adele gasped and clapped her hands over her face as she sank to the ground, Bella reached out to her and stroked her back gently, feeling each individual sob rack her body. Bella's heart sank, not due to her own feelings or the fate of her parents but for the pain her sister was feeling. It took a while for it to sink in that the psychopath that had been tormenting them for weeks was their brother, who thought he had it bad.

Moments passed slowly as they hid behind the cart, praying not to be caught, they wondered whether it was done, if their parents were dead. They were waiting for the crowd to cheer or boo or whatever people did at hangings. But that sound never came because the main gate exploded into thousands of tiny pieces with a sound that made every bone in the body pound and throb. The girls were only alive because of the cart, they were thrown back by the force of the blast and flying debris from the gate and lifesaving cart.

Bella sat up, her ears ringing, her white gown ruined by dust and blood. She checked on Adele who was covering her ears with both hands and sobbing still, tears streaking her dusty face.

Bella craned her head over the debris and squinted her eyes to see through the cloud of dust that billowed from the hole where the gate was. Through the dust cloud she could see people marching through the gate, Bella stood up to get a better luck at the intruders.

She could just make out noises from the courtyard, people screaming inaudible words, the slapping of guard's feet on the cobbles slowly approaching.

"BELLA!" A voice screamed from the chaos. She searched for the voice in the dust cloud but couldn't make out the owner of the voice, was it someone from the Guild? She pulled a still sobbing Adele to her feet, she wiped the tears from her older sisters face and gripped her hand tightly in her own. Adele smiled.

"Quite the distraction, eh?" She joked.

"BELLA!" The voice screamed again, closer this time, Bella could barely make out that it was a man's voice. *Charlie?*

"Who the hell?" Adele asked, but Bella just began hobbling into the dust cloud in search of the voice, her sister reluctantly trailing behind her. The two factions were nearly upon each other and the great battle was about to start, that was when she saw him. She raced towards him as fast as she could with her cast and crutches and threw her arms around him.

"Bells, oh my god, you are alive!" Will breathed into her hair, hugging her tightly. "I brought your knives, and sword. It's a shame actually... I was really getting used to them." He joked, beaming brightly. She smiled and kissed him, taking him by surprise. She hadn't stopped thinking about that kiss before the fight and she wished she'd told him how she felt, being imprisoned for weeks really put life into perspective. She broke apart from him, leaving him staring dumbstruck, mouth slightly agape as she took her weapons from him. She had said that he could have them if she died and she hoped he was overjoyed that he hadn't inherited them. Bella strapped her trusty knives around her body and sat on the ground. Adele just hovered shyly behind her, wondering what the hell was going on, Will only noticed her when Bella sunk to the ground and began hacking away the cast that had been the bane of her life.

"Oh hey, I'm Will from the Assassins Guild." He said and politely offered her his hand to shake. She shook it sceptically.

"My name is Adelaide and I'm Mar... Bella's sister, nice to meet you. So, what's the plan?" She said equally as politely. Will was shocked for a moment but recovered himself quickly, he handed her a sword and breastplate from a wagon they had brought in. She put them on reluctantly. Charlie finally caught up with his son, the rest of the assassins streaming behind him.

"Ah the sister! Charles. I didn't think we'd ever find you." Charlie said, extending his hand to Adele. She shook it, politely glazing over the comment she didn't understand.

The battle was in full swing now, with assassins and the resistance using swords, knives, bows and explosives. Whatever they could scrounge up, most of which was blunt and old, having been hidden for years, just in case. The assassins had managed to amass a following of about four hundred men and women on their march from the Guild, word spreading through secret whispers like wildfire reaching villages days before the assassins themselves. Charlie was especially proud of this fact as they had managed to do it and still sneak up on the *all-seeing* Castle. Although he was worried the Guild armoury couldn't provide protection for them all, the neighbouring villages resistance had taken what spare weapons and armour they had brought with them, those unlucky enough to have joined their march closer to the Castle had to rely on whatever they had laying around their homes at the time of departure.

It wasn't an understatement to say the Castle were much better prepared, they had modern weapons, guns of various calibres and cannons, strategically placed. All designed to withstand exactly this situation, not to mention the garrison of two hundred trained soldiers that resided at the Castle.

The resistance was at a disadvantage, they knew that going in but they were too pissed off to care, like all good resistances. They were bottle necked coming into their self-made entrance in the Castle wall which made them a high impact target for the Castles cannons. To combat this the resistance had ladders to mount the wall so that they could enter the compound from any angle.

The compound had been huge and pristine with its beautiful glass buildings and white cobblestone underfoot and walls, but now it was a battlefield, it was impossible to hear anything but war cries and the sound of gunfire. The white cobblestones were no longer white, the buildings were no longer beautiful, rivers of blood stained the cobbles pink and glass crunched awkwardly underfoot with every step.

"Okay, the plan was to take out the King, any idea

who that is? And where can we find him?" Will screamed over the battle.

"The courtyard! Our parents are there too, they were going to be hanged for treason before you guys came!" Adele screamed back.

"Okay, Bells you nearly done down there?" Will bent down and shouted in her ear. She nodded her head as she ripped the last part of the cast away, *a battlefield with only one shoe was going to be interesting*, she thought, *especially with all this glass around*. She stood up and despite everything, felt stronger than ever. "That's err quite the look, torn gown, one shoe, breastplate and knives." He said so only she could hear, she blushed and couldn't help but smile in return and pushed him forward towards the courtyard, towards the heated battle raging before them.

Together the three of them ran towards the courtyard picking up Charlie, Henry and the Ox on the way. Bella hadn't thought about it until now but they all must have graduated, that made her feel strangely sad, but happy that she was reunited with her friends once more. They slashed their way through a small party of Castle soldiers with ease, putting their training to good use. It felt good to release all the pent up energy and hatred Bella had stored up over the weeks of her imprisonment. She didn't hold back even though she was aware that her sister was watching her out of the corner of her eye, probably sickened at the obvious pleasure her little sister felt in the heat of battle, her enemies blood pooling at her feet and dripping down her sword arm. They stopped just short of the courtyard, where a cluster of buildings were untouched by the carnage.

"Okay, plan is to go in, kill the King and get out,

once we send word he is dead we will pull everyone out of the battle okay?" Charlie said authoritatively. "It's good to see you again Belladonna, I'm glad you're alive and found your family."

"Our parents are in there too, they were going to be hanged, can we rescue them too? Please." Adele said, her eyes pleading. Charlie's eyes skipped over to the courtyard and back to Adele.

"If we can, but the priority is the King." He said, he took the bow that was slung around his shoulders and knocked an arrow. "Let's go." Adele had explained to the group Abel's appearance and demeanour, to speed things up. Bella was conflicted by this whole situation, they wanted to save her parents that she had never met but kill her brother that turned out to be the King, who was also a sociopath. *Just go with it,* she told herself.

They stormed into the now empty courtyard and searched for any sign of Abel, Diane or Maxwell, but found nothing of any use. Evidence that people had left in a hurry were all around, items of clothing, walking sticks and even children's toys had been forgotten in the moment of panic that followed the explosion. They circled back to the entrance to the courtyard

"Where the hell are they?" Charlie snapped at Adele, Bella shot him a glance and he backed down.

"Check the throne room." Henry chipped in, they all looked at him.

"What?"

"If this guy is obsessed with power as you have made him out to be, then he will want his final stand to be in the throne room. His rightful place." Henry smirked, Charlie smiled and shook his head.

"God damn it, you're a smart kid Henry. Adele, any idea where there is a throne room?" Charlie asked.

"Not a throne room as you would imagine, but maybe the council's conference room?" She said doubtfully. The sounds of the battle around her made her feel very uncomfortable.

"Lead the way. Everyone, eyes peeled, stay on your toes." Will interrupted with the authority of his father, Charlie smiled.

When they arrived at the correct building Bella noticed that there were guards posted outside, *jackpot,* thought Bella. They wouldn't have spared guards in the middle of a battle to guard an empty building, they hid around the corner of a nearby building and came up with a plan.

"I say we use Adele as bait, she can distract the guards and then we take them out and work our way through the building." Will said bluntly. Bella punched him on the shoulder and scowled at him shaking her head. She didn't like the sound of that idea, she wanted to keep her sister out of harm's way.

"Bella, it's a good plan. The guards know me and if I take this gear off then they won't suspect a thing, they'll think I need saving. I can be bait. Easy." Adele said honestly to her sister. Bella looked around the circle and no one would meet her gaze, looks like they were all thinking the same thing. She gave in. Adele handed over her breastplate and sword to Will, she stood for a second with her eyes closed preparing herself. When she opened them there were tears rolling down her dust stained cheeks and she looked distraught.

"Great acting, could give you a run for your money Bells." Whispered Will. Bella patted Adele on the arm and she set off towards the building running slowly and pretending to catch her breath. They could barely make out what she was saying to them, but they seemed to buy it and turned to let her in.

"Now." Charlie whispered, he loosed his arrow and the Ox her crossbow bolt. Both found their targets, the small eye slit in the guards helmets. The only weakness in the whole armour, the ammo buried themselves into the guards unsuspecting eyes and they slumped to the ground metallically. Adele put her hands over her mouth to suppress a scream, no one told her how much blood there would be. She gathered her nerves once more to seem strong in front of her sister and their band of assassins. Will and Henry dragged the bodies inside and put them out of sight while the rest of them made their way up to the first floor.

"You know the drill." Charlie said as he led them up the first flight of stairs, an arrow knocked apprehensively. Bella had her knives at the ready and walked in front of Adele like a human shield, Adele was followed by Will with his sword poised ready to engage, Henry followed Will and the Ox brought up the rear with her crossbow. Single file they swept the first floor, taking out any soldiers they came across, they were mainly posted at the entrance to the stairwells. They swept the second and third floors in the same fashion but found no sign of Abel or the other Kings. Bella was starting to feel anxious, she had a feeling her parents were already dead, and Abel had escaped.

They paused before the fourth floor because they heard voices of soldiers, laughing about how they had managed not to be in the thick of the battle. Oh how they would wish that's where they were when they encountered the bunch of assassins lying in wait on the stairwell.

Bella, Charlie (with his dagger) and Will charged into the room and took out three soldiers immediately, there were six others sat around startled by the sudden attack. It took them a second to register what was happening, by this point it was too late for them as the Ox took one more down with her crossbow, Bella threw knives into two of the closest guards' necks with alarming precision. Will charged in and slashed the gun out of another's hand before he had time to fire it and then pulled a dagger out of his boot plunged it into the soldier's chest, piercing the weak chainmail. Charlie gracefully vaulted the tables and finished off the two furthest away with a dagger, sword combo. Henry had stayed behind in the stairwell to watch over Adele, which was a sensible idea as Bella didn't want her to see what she was capable of.

"Someone taught you well." Joked Charlie like a proud mother hen.

"Behind you!" Shouted Will, Charlie immediately spun around into another soldier who had emerged from the next room, the gunshots echoed through the room as Charlie knocked the gun upwards with the flat of his sword. But it was too late the bullets hit their target. They hit Charlie's armour and ricocheted off into Will's leg, a light shattered, and their sneaky advantage was demolished. Charlie followed the bullet's path with his eyes and gasped. Bella threw her last knife into the soldier's chest, making the soldier drop her gun and collapse to the floor, blood gushing through her shaking fingers from the fatal wound in her chest.

Henry and Adele burst into the room at the sound of gunshots and saw the aftermath of the fight, Will was stood stunned by the unfamiliar wound in this leg leaking blood quickly down his leg, Charlie sprinted across the room to his son and Bella stood wide eyed and crazed. Adele swooped across the room after seeing the bullet wound.

"You guys go, they'll be on the move now. I know how to deal with this, Henry will stay with me. Alright?" Adele barked her orders. Henry nodded. Charlie looked reluctant for a second to leave Will but nodded in agreement with the rest of them. Bella bent down to the panicked Will and cupped his face in her hands, the look on his face pained her, he was scared. For the first time in his life he was scared, and it was plastered all over his face. She placed a lingering kiss on his forehead and smiled encouragingly. He managed a weak smile of his own in return and she left him lying bleeding on the floor with her sister as his nurse. Her gut sank as she left the room, collecting her knives from her victims as she went, wiping their blood on her already bloodstained white gown. She had a bad feeling about this, the two people she had ever cared for in one room, at the same time, without her there. She swallowed her anxieties and followed Charlie up the stairs to the next floor.

Chapter Fourteen
Ultimatum

The remainder of the assassins snuck up the stairs, if anyone had heard gunshots on the floors above they certainly didn't act like it. Maybe they were waiting to ambush them, who knew. They reached the stairwell door and took a breath. They were all poised ready to fight, there were only three of them left now but they were all trained assassins, so they still had a better chance than most.

"Go in, clear as many as possible and then we will deal with your parents because let's be honest they are going to use them to get to you Bella. This attack is so much bigger than you and them, this fight is years overdue. I can't guarantee they will live. I'm sorry." His eyes were swimming with emotion, his words were true. She nodded in agreement, she didn't know her parents that well and from what she had heard they weren't the best. If she could save them she would but like Charlie said she wasn't going to put the whole mission in danger because of it. They were about to make a move when they heard movement on the stairs, they all turned ready to fight the approaching people.

"Theo? Griff? What the hell are you doing here? You said you didn't want to be a part of this." Charlie blurted at the other heads of the assassins.

"We came to help you dummy, if you are going to put our organisation in danger we at least need to make sure you win. And we went to find reinforcements." Said Griff in his usual sassy tone. "Hey, you found the girl." He winked his hello at Bella. Behind them were at least a dozen of the contracted assassins from the guild all head to toe in black and steel. Theo nodded awkwardly to Bella.

"That was a good fight, I'm glad you made it." Was all he said.

"Okay the plan is we storm the room, take out as many as we can, be careful though they may have hostages and their guns are formidable, be careful." Charlie said as he prepared to burst into the room. The conference room was huge and spread over the most part of a whole floor in the building, so being cramped wasn't something Bella worried about as she looked at the hoard of assassins behind her.

They tore into the room weapons at the ready, there was only one person in the room. Abel.

"Ah so nice of you to make it, ooh and I see you brought friends. Dear sister there's nothing you can do." Abel goaded from the other side of the room, Bella sent a knife flying in his direction, but it stopped short of her brother, instead it just sparked and cracked menacingly as it met an electric field.

"Coward!" Shouted Charlie. "Come out from behind your shield, usurper and face us like a man." Charlie barked.

"Oh no, no, no my dear Charles I can't do that, you don't want to kill me, see. I have taken the liberty of putting a few... safety measures in place." He flicked on the screen next to him to reveal a line of people against a wall court martial style with a line of soldiers pointing their guns at them. They could just make out some of the figures, Diane, Maxwell, Declan, an elderly lady... Will, Adele and Henry. *God damn it! It was a trap!* "Kill me and they all die. It's your choice."

"Just kill the pansy." Shouted Griff at his usual volume. Charlie turned around and whispered to Theo.

"Sneak out with the rest of the assassins and stop *that* from happening and we will keep him talking." Charlie ordered in a whisper, Theo nodded dutifully and quietly led the band of assassin's downstairs.

"Abel, come on. You wouldn't kill her, would you?" Charlie said, stepping further into the room.

"Charlie, you really doubt how far *I* would go for self-preservation?" Abel chuckled.

"She. Raised. You." Charlie spat. She had never seen him get this emotional before, she stepped closer to the monitor to get a better look at the screen, to get a better look at the elderly woman they were discussing. It was Hazel. *How was she still alive? What is going on here?* Bella thought as she watched the events unfolding.

"No!" Abel screamed, "She raised you! She tolerated me…" He turned his back on Charlie and looked out of the big glass window.

"She loved you like a son, and I loved you like a brother Abel. Why would you do that to her, to us? My son is down there. You'd have him killed as well?" Charlie said getting ever closer to the place where the electric barrier was.

"No, no, no, nooooo! You are trying to trick me, they said you would. They said you would." Abel babbled manically. Charlie edged closer still, but Bella's eyes were fixed on the screen. She could see Theo and his band slowly making their way towards the soldiers, quietly taking out anyone in their way. It was just Bella and Charlie left upstairs so the force of sixteen assassins should be able to pull that off without any casualties on their side.

"Abel, look at me." Charlie said carefully, "Put down the barrier, I'm not going to hurt you. I couldn't risk it. You are my brother. Tell me who *they* are, and I can help you."

"No, they told me this would happen. I can't tell you who they are otherwise they will kill and replace me. Don't you see that this is all futile, I am not the biggest fish in the pond Charlie, I never was. They put me on this throne when I was just fifteen years old. I don't know what I'm doing. I was just trying to make sure no one questioned my rule, they said if I was usurped I wouldn't have their protection anymore. I shouldn't have left. I shouldn't have left." Abel rambled. Pressing his hands against the cool glass therapeutically. Charlie turned around to Bella and gestured for her to go downstairs to the others. He turned back to Abel before she had the chance to move. She watched them interact for a couple of seconds more, like a game of emotional tennis.

Bella bounded down the stairs knowing no one was left in the building, knowing she no longer had eyes on either situation. *Why did she leave Charlie with that psychopath? Why did she leave Adele and Will? Why does everyone have messed up families in this place?*

She ran as quickly as her tired and injured leg would take her, across the compound to near the main gate where everyone was. She got there just as Theo and the gang were behind the soldiers, she held her breath. She was still running, one of the soldiers turned around at the wrong time and saw Theo sneaking up behind him. It all happened in slow motion. The assassins moved in, not before the more trigger-happy soldiers had loosed a few bullets. Adele grabbed Hazel and pulled her to the ground, the Ox got hit in the arm and roared viciously.

Bella didn't see what happened to the others as she

was too busy running, she heard noise behind her as more soldiers came to join in, she drew her sword and slashed through them, trying to stop them reaching her friends. She ran on, flanked by enemy soldiers until she reached them. She collapsed by Will who was bleeding profusely from several fresh bullet wounds. Tears rolled down Bella's face. *No, no, no, no, no! This can't be happening.*

"Hey Bells, you made it." He sputtered, blood soaking his clothes. She leaned down and stroked his face, tears falling onto his dusty and bloodstained face. "I'm sorry Bells, I'm so sorry." She wanted to tell him how she felt, she wanted to tell him he couldn't die on her, not now, not when they are so nearly free and clear. That she wanted to spend the rest of their lives together, not just the rest of his life. She pulled his face close to hers and sobbed, feeling his warm racking breaths on her face comforting her.

"I'm sorry, I didn't write you my memoirs before I died." He laughed, his eyes shining through the layers of dirt and blood. She smiled through the tears. *He was really going to die, wasn't he?* She pressed her hands against his bullet wounds and willed them shut, trying to preserve his life. Someone was pulling her away, but she clung on. She wanted to scream at them to let her go, she wanted to say goodbye.

No, no, no, he's still alive. Get off me…. NOOOOOO!

But they tugged harder, whoever it was they were much stronger than she was.

"NOOOOOOOOOOOOO! GET OFF ME! GET OFF!" And the tugging stopped, everyone around her stopped, the hands grabbing her had fallen away. She looked around at the people near her and they all had their mouths agape. She'd spoken.

Seemingly unfazed by this Charlie was the first one to break the silence. "We need to go, Abel is dead, it is pure chaos. We need to leave. Now!" Charlie shouted next to her, he had been the one grabbing her, trying to pry her away from his sons' body. Everyone around her bustled and began to move but Bella just stood, the world went silent around her, her head was spinning along with the chaos of the world.

Nothing would ever be the same again, the whole world had been turned upside down in one afternoon.

And Belladonna had found her voice.

Chapter Fifteen
The Aftermath

After the battle at the Castle the band of revolutionaries and assassins fled, no match for the bullets and hi-tech weapons of the Castle guard. With Abel dead, the world was unknowingly, but not for long, thrust into chaos. With no-one to lead the people and stop other nations from invading. The extent of the recent prison break would change the course of history forever, unbeknownst to Bella and the others.

She was dragged from the broken castle wall and into the woods, people screaming at the ensuing gunfire that had chased them into the trees. If only they knew that their King was dead, they wouldn't be shooting at his two siblings and technically, heirs.

"Hurry! Run!" Adele screamed at Bella, but Bella didn't want to run or to hurry anywhere. She wanted to curl up in a ball and shut her eyes and wake up at the Guild with everything as it was before, with Will asleep in her chair, his chest rising and falling gently.

Charlie had picked her up at some point, her small frame shuddering uncontrollably against his body with every stride. He said nothing, he just kept running. Running away from the guards shooting at them. Running away from his son's body. Running.

They ran for what seemed like forever to Adele, her lungs were bursting, screaming for air and her legs were threatening to buckle underneath her with every stride. Everyone was feeling the same, exhausted and too scared to stop running, even though they hadn't heard gunfire in nearly an hour.

Finally they stopped when Charlie, who was leading

them, stopped. He gently placed Bella down at the foot of a large oak tree, it's roots reaching up and embracing her the way only a mother could. He signalled to the remaining assassins who'd been dragging and carrying the injured revolutionaries with them, like Charlie had with Bella. They disappeared into the woods. *Where the hell are they going,* thought Adele, when it hit her *they didn't think we were safe yet, they're probably setting up a perimeter and making sure we weren't followed.*

"What are we doing?" Said a nearby revolutionary, voicing what everyone was thinking. Adele turned to where Charlie had disappeared into the thicket of trees.

"Rest!" She addressed the crowd of bloody, battered and exhausted people. People who had helped her escape her prison of eight years, kingless people who were in need of a leader. "We will plan our next move, figure out where it is safe and go from there. Rest!" She preached, seeing the tired faces nodding back at her, too exhausted or injured to argue. She turned to the nearest revolutionary and asked.

"Do we have a doctor amongst us? Some people could do with medical attention before we move on." She said, emanating authority.

"I don't know Miss, but I'll find out." He said and was gone a moment later. *Was this how Abel felt when he was King?* She thought and half horrified at the thought pushed it away. She turned back to her sister, who was still laid where Charlie had put her. She slowly approached in a way you would an injured and unpredictable wild animal.

"Hey there." Adele said softly, reaching out to rub Bella's shoulder. She didn't pull away from her older sister's touch, she didn't do anything, she just sat and stared into space. Adele gave it a minute more, her hand lingering on Bella's torn tunic.

"You have your voice back." She probed softly. Bella snapped out of her trance, like she could hear for the first time since she heard the life leaving Will's body, in heart breaking gurgling.

"I…" Bella began, her voice hoarse from screaming. "I remember everything." Adele looked at her sister with a mixture of shock and fear on her face.

"You do?" She said, finally. Bella nodded with a look of grief on her face.

"I remember…" Bella chucked, her voice was warm like honey, bright and tuneful like a songbird. Just how Adele remembered it. "I remember when we were young and Mom and Dad, they, they used to take us camping in these woods. The council hated it, and said it was too unsafe."

"Yeah that's right, we'd have a campfire and Dad would tell these scary stories. Do you remember those? He'd tell us about the things that were out in the woods at night that would eat young princesses who misbehaved." Adele said, smiling with tears streaming down her face.

"I remember." Bella replied, thinking back to that clearing all those years ago on the first day of her new life, remembering fearing the darkness and the entities that resided in it.

"They didn't make it." Adele said, breaking the silence.

"What? Who?" Bella replied, eyes searching the crowd of battle worn faces.

"Mom and Dad." Adele said, choked up slightly. "There was an explosion, as we were leaving. They didn't make it." She repeated, trying to make it real for herself as well as her sister. Bella sighed and put her head in her hands. *They were nearly out, we saved them from execution,* she thought, *how many more people have to die before I can live a normal life?*

"I'm sorry." Adele said.

"It's not your fault, don't worry about it." Bella said through her hands. She raised her head and met her sisters searching eyes. "It's my fault, I shut down, I didn't protect them. It's my fault."

"No, no way! You were in shock, grieving! You got all your memories back in one go, there was nothing you could have done." Adele replied defensively. Bella shook her head. Adele slumped down beside Bella and softened her expression.

"You loved him?" She said.

"Yes." Bella replied, tears pricking in her eyes. "What happens now?" She said in an attempt to steer the conversation away from the dead boy she was grieving for.

"Well *Princess,* I have a feeling the fighting isn't done yet." Adele replied. Bella's resolve hardened. *The fighting isn't done yet*, she thought.

www.blossomspringpublishing.com

Printed in Great Britain
by Amazon